PRAISE FOR
THE EXHIBITION OF PERSEPHONE Q

A NEW YORK TIMES BOOK REVIEW EDITORS' CHOICE
AND WALL STREET JOURNAL AND VOGUE MOST
ANTICIPATED BOOK OF 2020

"Stevens's dreamlike first novel is a delicate and drifting exploration of Percy's relationships with friends, lovers, neighbors, and the many not-quite strangers who form the fabric of city life. As Percy wanders, New York itself is reflected through the prism of her many identities . . . in luminous prose that captures the essence of a place in the middle of its most defining transformation. A stellar debut."

Kirkus Reviews (starred review)

"Stevens's writing proves that both time and technology are best understood in retrospect, sequences made logical long after each moment has passed. The novel has a romantic slowness, unfurling gracefully, little by little, to show how quickly the present gives way to the future, or concedes to the past."

Haley Mlotek, *New York Times*

"I was magnetized not just by a great story, but one that felt uncannily timely . . . Percy is forced to confront questions of identity and selfhood that feel both poignant and meta during a time of crisis."

Michael Baron, *Literary Hub*

"Jessi Stevens is the Muriel Spark of 21st century New York."

Joshua Cohen

"Stevens has combined the surreal with the actual to create a book painfully relevant to this new age of female testimony . . . A fantastic debut."

Noelle McManus, *Women's Review of Books*

"A mordantly funny requiem for the early 21st century."
Publishers Weekly

"It's as if *The Big Short* were set in the dreamworld of Rachel Ingalls's *Mrs. Caliban*."
Audrey Wollen, *New York Times*

"You might not think Occupy Wall Street and prophetic garden gnomes would fit together within the confines of the same narrative. Now, here's Jessi Jezewska Stevens's new novel *The Visitors* to make the case that, yes, the two can mesh together seamlessly. It's the kind of ambitious, madcap narrative combination that's all too rare nowadays."
Tobias Carroll, *Tor.com*

"The book accepts, and even delights in, the strenuous absurdity of its characters' efforts to index the relationship between the virtual and the material, or to locate the source of reality in imagination."
Daisy Hildyard, *The Guardian*

"Here is a refreshing novel by an author willing to take chances . . . *The Visitors* stands as a pensive and important work . . . rare and exciting company."
Necessary Fiction

"It's both a bold, imaginative play on very recent history and a trenchant prophecy of the terrifying times we're collectively staring down the barrel of."
Anna Cafolla, *The Face* Summer Reads 2022

"Jessi Jezewska Stevens's frighteningly brilliant new novel *The Visitors* is both a bold reimagining of the recent past and an all-too-likely prophecy of what's to come. Caustic, intimate, and consistently surprising, this novel cements Stevens's place as one of the great chroniclers of our cruel and terrifying times."
Andrew Martin

Ghost Pains

Jessi Jezewska Stevens

SHEFFIELD – LONDON – NEW YORK

First published in 2024 by And Other Stories
Sheffield – London – New York
www.andotherstories.org

1 3 5 7 9 8 6 4 2

ISBN: 9781913505844
eBook ISBN: 9781913505851

Editor: Jeremy M. Davies; Copy-editor: Bella Bosworth; Proofreader: Sarah Terry;
Typesetter: Tetragon, London; Typefaces: Albertan Pro and Linotype Syntax
(interior) and Stellage (cover); Series Cover Design: Elisa von Randow, Alles Blau
Studio, Brazil, after a concept by And Other Stories; Author Photo: Nina Subin.

And Other Stories books are printed and bound in the UK on FSC-
certified paper. The covers are of G . F Smith 270gsm Colorplan card,
which is sustainably manufactured at the James Cropper paper mill
in the Lake District, and are stamped with biodegradable foil.

A catalogue record for this book is available from the British Library.

And Other Stories gratefully acknowledge that our work is
supported using public funding by Arts Council England.

For S.

CONTENTS

THE PARTY

The party was a failure. I can't even tell you what a failure it was. There are no words. Only a great pain in my chest when I wake up. On the veranda. It's better when I sit in the chair. Oh, but then I can see around. The gauzy curtains, pushed by the breeze! The glasses on the floor. Little ghosts! Last night the American walked around sniffing at them like a dog. He said, Who would leave all these dead soldiers behind? I couldn't say. I am American as well, but lately I haven't been feeling quite myself.

It's not the sort of thing I do, hosting parties. The last time I hosted anyone but Ann? It must have been months and months ago. It would have been Ann and her sister and her sister's friend. We ate schnitzel with *Kartoffelsalat* and plenty of pilsner, of course. The sister's friend was confused over the nature of his relationship to Ann. There was an ambiguity there. It ended in disaster. There's always an ambiguity with Ann—he should have known. I lost a perfectly nice vase that night and afterward I said to myself, Never again will I host even the smallest of parties. So who knows where it came from. The sudden urge. To invite everyone I know for drinks.

What a mistake! I was out here on the veranda, by the basil plant, as I often am when visited by caprice. I was by the basil plant having a smoke and thinking of the people in my life, specifically of Sylvia and the way she lights up a room in her light-blue dress. The bluebell sleeves that drape petal-thin over the styles of her arms. The way she holds a glass. With Sylvia it's always elegance. When she stands in a Berlin apartment, by a window, it is as if the world has traveled back in time. The haute bourgeoisie—they would feel right at home at her wonderful soirees, where the light is always kind of blue and the rooms reverberate with rumors. The low murmurs of a great many people drift fashionably through the floor. They are predicting the future, maybe. The future is happening now. The future is happening and here you are, right in the middle of it: a bit of ash falls to the carpet and then a great work of art has been achieved. Or will soon be achieved. No matter that tomorrow, on the street, we are hardly artists at all. In T-shirts and jeans. Not up to much good. Freelancers. We work at flat-screen monitors, designing advertisements at hotel desks, because it doesn't belong to you, does it, the desk isn't yours. The following week it could belong to someone else. "Dead soldiers." "Hotel desks." As phrases they conjure a kind of elegance, though not as well as Sylvia can whenever she hosts one of her parties. And it's quite possible it was Sylvia I was channeling out there by the basil plant last Friday when I resolved to throw a party myself. To feel, for a moment, as if my name were Sylvia. Or maybe Carlotta would suit. I tapped ash into the basil plant. If my name were Carlotta, I wouldn't have done that, you see. I would have had a proper ash-tray I picked up at some street market in southern Turkey, through whose haphazard aisles I had ventured on my own (so I'd tell my friends over cocktails) without even a scarf on my head. Because if my name were Carlotta, I wouldn't have to follow other people's rules. And my ashtray would be most divine. The basil plant was wilting. I caressed its leaves. I stamped my black ash into its soil. Then I set to work on my party, and I blame Carlotta for that. She lies. She ought to have dissuaded me. Sweetheart, she should have said, we're not the same.

Email! The way all modern tragedies begin. I copied the list of recipients Sylvia had used for her last party. Then I made a butter sandwich. *Liebe Freunde*, I wrote, You are invited to the following celebration tomorrow at 8 p.m. I reviewed the list of invitees. I made a second sandwich. "Siri," I said. "What's the email for the *Staatsbibliothek* man?" She didn't know. What's the email for the American? For the Swede? I was really quite swept up in the Swede, though he broke my heart whenever we met by speaking of Sylvia the whole time. And of course I added Ann. She was first on the list. Oh, Ann. Even Sylvia dims a little by comparison. That's Ann's special talent—she dulls all the luster and leaves you groping about in the dark. We can sit for hours on the veranda, not talking, Ann and I. Chewing basil leaves. She says to me, You know Yugoslavia isn't a country anymore? Quite right. She keeps it folded up inside her like a flag.

I went to make myself a third butter sandwich, but halfway through I lost my appetite. And then I was out of bread.

Really there's no need for parties anymore. There never was. I can go for weeks without speaking to anyone but Ann and the cashiers at the BioMarkt. And occasionally my phone. What a stupid woman, Siri must think, who has to ask for directions all the time. I followed her across Maybachufer Straße to buy a bag of almonds. One can always trust an almond, especially the Jordan type. The BioMarkt is another story altogether—I never know what to buy. I stood in the aisles and stared at the labels for *Maultaschen*. And *Apfelsaft*. For egg noodles. What does a party need? But you can only be so ridiculous in public, asking your phone for answers all the time. I bought bread and chocolate. I bought a large bag of grapes. Twelve apples. And popcorn. I hadn't seen it in a while. The kind you make in a pot. Not long ago I'd attended a Futurist dinner party some other girls threw featuring deconstructed spaghetti that spilled over tables and onto brown paper on the floor: here a pile of languid noodles; here a red lake of sauce. Well-dressed people crouched for fistfuls, hand to mouth. People have only just stopped talking about that party. It's still on everyone's mind. I imagined my bedroom filling with bowls and bowls of popcorn. Like snow. Like scatter art. I bought vodka and gin and plenty of apple juice, plus a liter of Club-Mate. Then it was back to my apartment, where I lit a cigarette and opened my email. No one had responded to my invitation but Ann.

Berlin has a habit of taking your life and smashing it back in your face. The Swede says that's how it is in New York, but I completely disagree. The way I remember it, New York does its face-rubbing out in the open, by the light of day, while Berlin strikes at the loneliest hour, in the dead of night, when the emotion is most dense, when the dogs come out to fight their arbitrary fights. The evening fell like a sigh. I watched it from my veranda. The light fading, the voices echoing the way they do when people start disappearing into bars. I turned around. I looked into my rooms. The green chair. The chandelier left over from some other life. The French doors, open, framed the groceries on the table. The popcorn. The grapes. The apples waiting to be sliced. The melancholy of a lemon—! I have always harbored an envy for Dutch still life. The apples went into a bowl. The grapes. The bottle of Club-Mate shone like a polluted moon. I laid out forks and plates and knives and there it was, a whole banquet set for one. Or many—for all my ghosts and me. I popped a whole pot of popcorn and ate it all. I could hear the people stumbling through the courtyard out the window. The scavengers are out there, every night. On the ground floor is a halfway house and people wander in and out. *Ich wohne hier!* they say, insistent yet uncertain. I could hardly blame them—I felt very half-hearted myself. I didn't feel like a Carlotta at all. To put it another way, I was reverting to myself. A woman alone with too much fruit. I'd have to invite Ann to help finish it all. Maybe tomorrow. We'd sit here eating grapes until all the grapes were gone. I opened the invitation I had sent. A change of plans. Due to an unforeseen scheduling conflict . . . *Send.* Then I lit a cigarette to burn away the shame. Every email makes me ashamed, it is inherent to the process. Send an email. Feel shame. Light a cigarette, like striking a match after taking a shit. "Dear Siri," I said. "Where's Ann?" "I'm sorry, I can't help with that right now." I heaved my heaviest sigh. My impossible life is always more impossible when Siri will not help.

By the way, I should explain about the dog. The day I decided to host the party I hadn't heard from it in weeks. Of course at first I didn't know it was a dog. My very first night in Berlin, I lay in my bed listening to the dubstep, the garage rock, the sound of people shuffling around the courtyard in the dark. The windows were open and the breeze was cool and fresh. I closed my eyes. I was very tired. I might have even slept. Then the night was torn by the most terrible scream. I sat up. The scream belonged to a very throaty woman or else a very young man. It rang and rang and then abruptly silenced. I waited. I expected a crash, the commotion of other people coming to the rescue. But there was no sound, everything was still. No one was helping at all. I stepped onto the veranda and looked up and down the boulevards, where the sidewalks were very empty. I went back to bed. Then the scream tore loose again.

Months like this! Imagine. I consulted Ann. What should I do? She suggested calling social services, but where would I tell them to go? I had no idea where the scream was coming from. It occurred to me it might even be of pleasure, not of pain. It was possible.

Especially in Berlin. Every night I lay awake examining the quality of the pleasure-terror. I tried to read its origins. Fear or pain or ecstasy. I became a student of screams. I recorded them. "Siri," I said, "play that back." I composed a whole symphony for Ann. We listened on the U-Bahn, sharing gluey earbuds. The sound was weak but it was there. Every night? Every night. She was quiet. The earbud hung parasitically from her lobe. She shook her head. "I don't know what to say," she said. Meanwhile I couldn't sleep. I alerted the landlady, who only shrugged. "I am not hearing this scream," she said. "You Americans. So fussy." After that I thought maybe it was only me. Something I heard in my mind. That only made the sleeping worse—I was afraid to go to bed.

One night I decided to put the landlady's theory to the test. To follow the scream. To see if it led back to me. I brought a flashlight and plenty of cigarettes. And Siri. I told her, "Be ready for an emergency call." I walked along the canal to the park. Looped back again. It was nearing two o'clock, when the scream usually began. I passed almost no one. The dealer was sitting by the footbridge, dealing weed. I don't have any money, I said, but have you heard the scream? He looked at me as if I were the suspicious one. I walked away. In the park I sat on a bench and waited. I wondered if the landlady had been right all along. A woman walked her dog and I wished that I were her instead. The dog was small and white, a lapdog, a really superfluous-looking pet. The woman let it trot freely across the lawn. It sniffed a tree. A fence. Then it stopped at the base of a statue. And began to scream. I leapt from the bench. This tiny dog was staring at the statue and baring its teeth. It was the very scream I'd been looking for. The scream of a thousand people burning alive. At the stake. After a bomb. Only there were no bombs. No stakes. No armies marching in the streets. There was nothing around but the owner and her dog. Who could love such a creature? Knowing it held such a scream? After that I listened from my bed and knew the truth. Then the nights fell silent. Where could the dog have gone, I thought, as I drifted off to sleep.

On Saturday I woke up with a predictable sense of regret. About canceling the party. I had a long lie-in, staring at the fleurs-de-lis embossed on the tin ceiling. You could never afford a ceiling like that in America now, I thought. Not unless you were born beneath it. I slipped out of bed and into my robe. My favorite robe, my only robe. I always spend too much on lingerie. I have three dresses and thirty brassieres. I dress for myself, you might say. The bras are for me. The robe. I am a wraith, inhuman, alone in my room in chiffon hemmed with lace. I'm behind on my rent. Though it's worth pointing out that while a robe costing one month's habitation is an expensive robe indeed, rent in Berlin, if you know where to look, is extremely cheap.

For breakfast I had a cigarette, and the basil plant had ash. I wore my chiffon out on the veranda and watched the people passing in the street. They disappeared into the *Bäckereien*. For *Brötchen*. I read a little Adorno. I read some Rilke and made a mental note to visit all the libraries in Paris. From now on it was Rilke from whom I'd take my cues. I thought of going for a walk. Then I was reading again. Rilke did all the walking. It's possible I might leave the apartment more, I thought, if I didn't own so much elegant lingerie.

I was still sitting there on the veranda, in the robe, when evening fell. I was thinking I ought to see Ann. Give her a call. See if she might help me finish the vodka and the fruit for the party I wouldn't have. Then it occurred to me that I might have already called her. This happens sometimes. I think of something I've already said as if I've never said it before—I blame Adorno. The illusion of the new. When really it's all just kitsch, it's all the same, everything's already been said and done. Then the doorbell rang, and I rejoiced: so I had called her after all! I tied off my robe and sifted down the stairs—that's the wonderful thing about chiffon, you do not walk but sift, you float—to the heavy wooden doors, expecting Ann, delighted about Ann, so grateful that no matter what happens I will always have Ann. But to my surprise, it was the American man. He was on the front step holding two half-liters of beer. "Where's Ann?" The American shrugged. "Nice dress," he said. And found his own way up the stairs.

Oh, the nuance of *reply* versus *reply all*! Not really so nuanced. Ann, the only guest to write back, was the only one to receive the cancellation: the perils of enthusiasm, incurred. I had in effect orchestrated the exact inverse of the evening I had planned. What a pity, Ann says, whenever anything goes wrong, no matter how disastrous. Her little Yugoslav heart! I could have used its support. I called but she didn't answer. Then I called again. Meanwhile the American was opening the door to my apartment with a hip. He's been here before, unfortunately—I'm afraid we had a tryst. The apartment was a mess. The apples and grapes and Club-Mate on the table, the table set for a banquet of ghosts. There was music playing somewhere, but in my apartment it was quiet. The doors to the veranda were open and the breeze was drifting through. The American opened the fridge and peered inside. It was empty save my collection of half-finished jams. "You did say tonight?" "Yes." The party was tonight. The American nodded—he is one of those men who uses silence to tell you what to do. Then he stationed himself at the kitchen table and quickly fixed himself a drink. Looked around. At the kitchen. At the veranda. At the unmade bed beneath its fleurs-de-lis. "Right," he said. "This won't do at all.

Do you have any glasses?" I pointed to the fleet of jam jars in the cupboard. Then I made the bed.

The American sliced lemons. Pale citrus rounds that gave my chest a pang. They sliced up my heart! He turned the radio on. It was all too similar to the last time he had been here, I thought, and he must have felt the same. He in the kitchen, I in my robe. The bed. Not talking. The radio on. I hadn't called the American since that night. I'd left him right here in the sheets, in fact, after he'd fallen asleep. I walked around, I smoked. I went to Ann's. He woke up all alone in my apartment. I heard from the Swede he was very upset. Now he was looking through the liquor bottles in a proprietary way and selecting Triple Sec, for punch. I stood in the French doors and watched as he poured the whole bottle into a bowl. I felt a wave of regret. "Why are you helping me?" The American answered without looking up. "National pride," he said. He tuned the radio dial and a popular song came on, the same one playing downstairs. It was the most popular song in the world. The Swede knew the person who wrote it. That's how it is in Sweden—it's a small country, in the end. The song played. I longed for the Swede. "Now we're cooking," the American said. He snapped his fingers. Good to go. On a roll. Then the doorbell rang. The American fixed his hair and smoothed his tie. "So go get it," he said. As if he were the host of the party.

Sometimes I think life is really just one long logic problem to be solved via process of elimination. Or perhaps that's just how you know that you are growing old. When each gathering becomes a complex series of equations and permutations and postulates about whose presence excludes whom: If X and Y cause a fight, and Z and X are sleeping together, and Z is also sleeping with A, who carries a knife, and A and Y must meet for work, whom do you invite to dinner so that everyone has a date? When you solve the word problem that is my life, the correct answer is no one at all, no two people can be in the same room at once. QED. What I mean to say is, I really should have checked that list of Sylvia's before copying it for purposes of my own. I had ignored this obvious precaution and now the apartment was filling with all the men I'd slept with, plus all the women they loved now or were sleeping with instead. The American. The Bulgarian. The Swiss. The Swede, who kept looking to the door every time someone new arrived. He was waiting for Sylvia, of course. I could have died. Instead, I did a lot of laughing. People kept arriving and I ran up and down the stairs to let them in. I acted as if I'd been drinking all day and didn't expect to make it through the night. As if I didn't notice that the men seemed to be purposely getting along extremely well while ignoring me, as if they'd established a whole nation of their own. I wanted to scream. The women were complimenting my robe as if it were a dress. Everyone was holding jelly jars. And jam jars. And jars for marmalade—I am always buying French preserves, you see, which come in the most luminescent shades, and which assume afterlives as tumblers for women in distressed jeans and glitter shoes, those sporty shirts that slide up the spine. The veranda! Completely full of fashionable people. I didn't know any of them. Then Sylvia arrived, and everything went still.

Oh Sylvia, I thought. Must there really be more than one of you?

Under any other circumstances I would have been flattered beyond belief that Sylvia had graced a party of mine. I would have taken her by the arm, by the wrist, and welcomed her in a perfect imitation of herself. But I was stunned stupid by the beauty of the girls that she had brought. I lost entire minutes of my life trying to make their loveliness compute. How easily they wore it, like lines in novels you never forget: *We carry death within us like a stone within a fruit* . . . The party swelled around the new arrivals, feeding on them like fish. I had to elbow my way through. Sylvia was basking in her own perfume. *"Bisou,"* she said, and bent to kiss my cheek. She almost seemed more beautiful by virtue of not being, technically, the most beautiful of all. The other girls were Platonic precedents for Sylvia herself. Sylvia: ideal woman in the flesh. She lifted the sleeve of my robe and let it fall with a trellised laugh. "Charming!" She explored my limbs as if she'd never seen anything like me before, a little mutant in chiffon. I should mention that the robe is quite transparent. As gauzy as the curtains and of a very light teal, like the copper patina of an old machine. What I'm saying is you can see right through it to my white balcony bra. Little rosettes fasten straps to cups. "So sweet," Sylvia said, fingering the appliqués. "You're a vision." She laughed again. "I want to be just like you!" The kind of thing you can say only if you're beautiful and French. Then she unzipped her slim and midnight jeans and stepped into the smooth suit of her skin, her long and lovely legs, the matching blue of her panties and bra. She walked across the room like a sea. I have often thought this of especially beautiful women, that they walk like the water through which everyone else wades. Everyone watched. The music stopped. She was so elegant, traveling through the dark. Like art. She accepted a drink. The music resumed. And all of a sudden the other girls were casually discarding clothes, as if this were the thing to do. As if we'd been served a kind of fairy-tale cue, midnight, for everyone to take off her dress. A moment before I had been barely clothed and now I was wearing more clothes than everyone else. I went around the room urging people to put their fashionable outfits on. "Oh, please. Put on your clothes." "Please," people said. "Take them off." They clawed at my chiffon. The party pushed me onto the veranda with a coordinated shove. There I found the basil plant. On the ground. Soil scattered like black blood. How horrible! A death! The oldest of my two true friends. Inside they were singing the world's most popular song. The Swede was drawing his tongue along Sylvia's slender neck even as she carried on conversations with nearly naked friends. "Look here," I said. "A death! Don't you see?" And then of course the night was usurped by the dog with the human scream.

It was back! I was filled with flutters of joy. The joy of recognition. For someone I thought I'd lost. I smiled. Not even the landlady could doubt me now. I looked around my apartment and saw the faces blank with fear. The girls in their bras. The men with their drinks. The chandelier glinted somewhere near the ceiling, and the screaming went on and on. The only pauses were for breath. What is it, they whispered. I wanted to explain. I wanted to tell them, Don't worry, it's all in your head, it's not your fault, it has nothing to do with you. But words failed me. I couldn't help it—I began to laugh. It could have been the Triple Sec, or maybe it was grief. I cradled the pot in my arms. A grave for the lopsided plant. I laughed and laughed. People started dressing. First very slowly. Then in a panic. Trading clothes. Putting on whatever came first. I laughed so hard it hurt. I bowed over the basil, drawing inward as I laughed. We were a chorus, the dog and I. Of pleasure and of pain. The women began to cry. In the bruise-blue dark I caught a glimpse of Sylvia struggling to fit a foot through her too-tight jeans. Her wide forehead pushed through the collar of a shirt. Someone larger pushed her aside. People were leaving all at once, they even left behind their drinks. I laughed them out. I didn't stop. Then it was only the American and me. And all the dead soldiers. Who would leave all these dead soldiers behind? He went around the room with a bag. He must have been deaf. I laughed myself to sleep. And then I woke up. Lit a cigarette. What a failure the party was. I almost miss the screams.

HONEYMOON

For our honeymoon we went to Tuscany. This got a big sigh from me. I love my job, this city, my life. At home, in our apartment, the kitchen floor tiles are ivory and deep maroon, a chessboard for girls. I was sitting on them, like a squat little knight, unwrapping a casserole dish, when my husband wheeled a suitcase into the room. One of the most interesting discoveries about being married, I find, is that those things you choose not to say out loud don't register at all. No one reads your mind. He gently snapped two fingers near my face.

"Babe," he said. "You look a little dazed."

The first thing I did when we arrived was set up my salves and creams and serums on the vanity. I laid out my hairbrush handle first. The tweezers. The tints. I like to keep everything in little rows, like soldiers ready for battle. It was Ciccro, I believe, who while on an Aristotelian riff proclaimed that the essence of style is *appropriateness with respect to time and place*. I looked at my platoon of jars. The bouquet of brushes. The glint of the sun on the edge of a cup. All at once it struck me as too much. Perhaps it wasn't so tasteful for a married woman to disclose all the secrets of her face. Perhaps she ought to keep some for herself. One by one, I replaced the vials and jars in their quilted armory. An air of mystery overtook the room. I was soothed. But the vanity looked rather spartan. Shouldn't there be a nail file or at least a tube of lipstick? I glanced at my husband, asleep on the bed. The shape of him. Half my vials returned to the stage before the mirror, though this, too, seemed a losing compromise. At dinner, I spooled spaghetti onto my fork. I ordered a Negroni—or three. It struck me that a partial vanity capitalizes on only half the virtues of femininity, while retaining all its vices.

To be fair, I can't really say that I enjoy vacations. In a sense I'm on vacation all the time, so when I'm away it feels like work. I am a jewelry consultant in the gift shop of a five-star hotel, where I tend to a nook filled with gems. (One works one's way up; my husband was a former guest.) All week long I daydream to the sound of heels clacking across a polished marble floor. I could be miles away. I could be at the beach! Occasionally the phone rings, and then there's some real excitement—a guest is placing an order for a surprise. The rest is a breeze. I take lunch twice. At two, I put a sign on the door and go for a jog. BE BACK SOON. No one seems to mind. Tuscany, likewise, was permanently on leave. Any direction I looked there was nothing but farms and hills and leisure time. A tractor churned. Someone opened a bottle of wine. The local cheese was Pecorino, and I wasn't sure I had a taste for it, though my husband liked it fine. As for me, I craved a bagel. I missed Christopher Street Chinese. Lo mein. Pot stickers, steamed. At least in Tuscany the cigarettes were very cheap. I had one in the evening. I had two. My husband looked up from his phrase book and asked, "Is this a permanent thing?" "Of course," I said. Because that's the modus operandi of a marriage, permanence. He smiled. We traipsed to the pool. We wandered through medieval towns sipping different wines. Sometimes we strolled the grounds. We made love. I slipped into a sequined dress with Cinderella sleeves for drinks, and in the morning, I woke up early and watched my husband breathing in the sheets, half expecting him to get up and leave. He didn't. Still, I dressed quietly so he would not be disturbed and change his mind. I slid on my shoes, my sweat-stained bra. I jogged.

On a Tuscan morning, Negronis linger; every step ricocheted inside my head. I followed the dirt road along the ridge for miles. The hangover grew worse and worse and then, suddenly, stopped. I breathed. I liked to jog early, before the sense of privacy could seep away like rainwater into the ground. At dawn, no one was around but the German tourists and the Milanese, who were always up, attending to their fitness. I saw them as I slogged over dusty crests, huffing heavily—I'm not used to hills. Fortunately the Germans seemed to prefer their mornings in the opposite direction. They were always going up when I was coming down.

It occurred to me, on those solitary treks, that what I truly missed was being engaged. Now there's a vacation. You can get away with anything when you're a fiancée. One day I was a bride-to-be. The next, a smoker. Shortly after that I started jogging—I had a lot of weight to lose to fit into my dress, which I'd ordered a size too small. Size six is a good size for a woman like me. My mother-in-law agreed. She is often agreeing with me, even as I'm not so certain, in the moment, whether I am agreeing with her. The jogging may even have been her idea to start—in any case, it's stuck.

On a nice day, warm, after a particularly long run, one wants nothing more than to lie on a balustrade by a river eating bright scoops of gelato with a tiny neon spoon. Instead we went to Florence, to the Uffizi. That old Medici palace, my husband had said, is where all the art is kept. I had a lot to learn. I stared into a room encrusted

23

with shells. I stared at Botticelli's Venus. She was also on the half shell, stubbornly still in the painterly suggestion of a wind. I caught an eyeful of camera flash. We drifted through the galleries. We paused before an Annunciation backdropped entirely in gold: the archangel kneels, Mary is on her throne. My husband punched a few numbers into his phone and held it to his ear. A small voice spoke to him. The Hail Mary, it said, was written directly on the painting. The prayer angled toward the Virgin like an arrow: *Ave Maria, gratia plena . . .* And Mary, she turned away. She pouted, haughty and unwilling. Of course she recoiled; it is the only reasonable response to unexpected advances by a stranger in the night. My husband and I admired her good sense in silence. I felt his fingers reach for mine. The audio guide whispered its sweet nothings. For a moment I wondered whether I, too, had settled for whatever had come along when I should have turned away. If so, I couldn't help it.

I'm no saint.

The next morning there was an accident. We were in the kitchen, making toast. My face was still flushed from my jog. My husband was burning through a box of matches, trying to light the stove. He struck. The blue tip fizzled. He struck again. He guided the small flame toward the burners. Then we heard a crash. The match missed and the stove hissed gas. We were quite alone in our villa, my mother-in-law being the kind of person with private villa connections to spare. Very private. The nearest neighbor was miles away.

At home, in the city, when the occasional roach shoots out from under the skirt of the couch, we take turns smashing it. We take turns taking out the trash. In this moment, however, there was no knowing whose turn it was. For a long while we did nothing at all.

Then my husband killed the gas and inched open the door. It was a big wooden drawbridge of a door. On the steps there was a bird. My husband looked at it. He looked at the door. He shook his head. Then we were in mourning, and I was ashamed, in the Ciceronian sense, of my bold mauve shirt.

The bird cast a pall over the short drive to Siena. Out the window, the landscape passed in smooth swaths of green and mud, faded because left out too long in the sun. My husband rubbed his face. "I don't understand," he said. He ran through the evidence. There wasn't any glass; the bird couldn't have mistaken its reflection for something else—like another bird. That's usually what happens, when birds fly into doors. I nodded. "I guess it was in the wrong place at the wrong time." My husband fell silent. He pulled to the side of a narrow road to let a tour bus pass. I studied the map. "Fifteen kilometers to Siena," I said. Then I looked up, only to be contradicted by a hand-painted sign: CHILOMETRI 25.

There is a great dignity problem for the tourist in Italy. Is there supposed to be a Giotto in here? Isn't the dick a little small? Doesn't Jesus look a little fat? I was afraid of saying something stupid. Everywhere we turned I saw ourselves: young couples in blister-proof shoes and fresh white shirts, holding hands, craning toward cathedral ceilings. Older couples, too, were everywhere, dreaming of home and separate rooms, where one can shut the door. They stared at us the way one stares into the past. There is a great dignity problem in getting married, I think. The problem is there in the garters, the flowers, the pictures, the pictures, the pictures, in your mother-in-law arriving with a tiny airbrush to hose away the contours in your face (and who knew you could brush away the contours of a female face? Botticelli, that's who, the Uffizi says), it is there in the size six dress you have to half unzip to keep eating cake because you don't want to dance. One is quite low on self-esteem following a wedding, and Tuscany is no help. I folded the map. To be both a newlywed and a tourist—it's the most undignified position of all.

In Siena, my husband took out the List. The List was compiled by a college friend of his with a Ph.D. in medieval studies. A personal travel guide, just for us. It was this same friend who told us, before we left, to walk into every church, which in practice had turned out to be a lot of work. It was physically and spiritually taxing to stand in line at every duomo, an exhaustion compounded by the subjects of the frescoes. Trapped in holy plaster, they emoted heavily, gazed over my shoulder to the vanishing point of sorrow. In Siena, however, I had new hope. The duomo was tiled in teal and pink. It looked more cheerful than most—but inside it was as dark and dim as ever. My husband stood in the nave and consulted the List, then pointed us toward Donatello's *Feast of Herod*, where there was already a crowd. We took our place in the throng. We stared for a while at the bronze relief, in which a kneeling man presents the head of John the Baptist on a plate. My husband whispered facts. "It's notable for its use of perspective," he said. I nodded. He said, "I guess John disapproved of Herod's marriage to his sister-in-law? That's why—you know." I did. What I didn't say was that it struck me people are always feasting just before a murder. Herod. Judas. My husband and I, as regards the bird. It brought to mind a copy of *The Last Supper* that hung in the cafeteria at school when I was a girl. It was a glossy, supersaturated print, installed above the entrance to the convent. I spent long minutes lost in its restorative reds and blues while waiting for second helpings of chicken nuggets. I'm not sure now whether it was the painting itself that conjured such an irresistible sense of mystery, or its proximity to the nuns' quarters, which we entered only very rarely, and where they tended to a sliver of the cross. A splinter of death.

They kept it on a satin pillow inside a plastic ring box. Imagine: a whole class of elementary students, sitting silent in the pews. When the relic came to me, I tried hard to see something grander than a piece of mulch. A needle of bark that might lodge itself, come summer, in the bottom of my foot. I sensed that everyone else was deeply impressed by this holy amulet. They held it tenderly, with awe. I tried to listen with my soul. It was no use. All my life I would have liked to believe. I would have liked to feel moved by the candles in the church, and the silence, and the priests slotted into catacombs underground. Only I couldn't concentrate, not as one among a crowd. In Tuscany the situation was much the same. I kept looking around. I got distracted by our collective struggle to renaissance ourselves. One cannot gawk one's way into personal transformation. And yet that seemed to be my main activity of late—I'm afraid I gawked all day.

Standing before *The Feast of Herod*, my husband was the one who looked a little dazed. He didn't seem to notice when two children sprinted between us, colliding with his legs. His mind was back on the doorstep of the villa. I took his hand. "Don't worry," I whispered. "I'm sure it didn't feel any pain."

At noon, in a Sienese bistro, tasting Pecorino cheese, making love could not have been further from my mind. How obscene! I felt so thoroughly a tourist, who would possibly want to have sex with me? Not my husband, surely. Then night fell. We drove home. The landscape was lush and promising; Tuscany returned. Any blemishes were airbrushed by the dark. Back at our villa, it was as if we, too, had transformed into different beings. We'd come home as strangers to our daytime selves. "Do you want a glass of wine?" my husband asked. Why not? We drank the whole bottle while considering the stars, discussing Herod. His vengeful wife, Herodias. Obedient Salome. Apparently they tricked him into demanding John the Baptist's head—my husband read aloud from the Wiki version on his phone. "It's all too extreme in the Bible," I said. "There's no room for ambiguity, and it's always a woman at fault." He lay back in the grass and pointed his phone at the sky, as if to image-search the constellations. Later that night I woke up to internal alarms. My husband heard them, too. We reached for each other through the film of sleep. After, we lay in the borrowed sheets, looking into the firmament of the bedroom ceiling, as quiet as we ought to have been when searching for that Giotto in the church. I told my husband the story of the convent's remnant of the cross. His face was a pale lantern in the dark, his voice as flat as bronze, no irony at all.

"Do you really think they had a sliver of the cross?"

In my line of work you get a sense for liars. The jewelry nook is a confessional, a place of transience and vulnerability, where what you're vulnerable to is yourself. Men come in with stacks of credit cards and leave with wedding rings and strings of pearls. My wife, they say. My girlfriend. My mother. My niece. I try to intervene. I try to make suggestions—sterling silver for a little girl?—but most seem pretty savvy on their own: pearls for the niece, white gold for the wife, diamonds for the mistress. It makes one wonder what a jewelry consultant like me is for. One afternoon, not long before we left for Tuscany, I marched upstairs to my manager's office to ask, What am I here for anyway? For whom do I consult? He drew his fingertips together and rested his elbows on the desk. "You're here," he said, "to facilitate a match." With all due respect, I told him, the matches seemed to make themselves. "Yes," he said, "but you create the opportunity, the air of receptivity. You create the space." Something like that. I went back downstairs. The way I understand it, I am an architect, and what I construct are invisible castles in which my tenants might receive the more beautiful objects of this life. These tenants are mostly men. I ask them, Why not get something for yourself? A few accept. They go straight for the cuff links. They ask, Can these be monogrammed? Lucky thing—they can.

My husband was a cuff-links man. His matched the glint of his drink as he sat in the lobby bar the day we met. I was on my break. They were very nice cuff links. I admired the stainless-steel setting and the understated crown: an amber fleck. He saw me staring and gave his wrists an ironic glance. "It's not my fault," he said. "My girlfriend bought them." And what was a man to do, he added, when meeting said girlfriend for drinks? I asked him whether she'd bought them here at the hotel. He shook his head. "Too bad," I said. We offered a ninety-day return policy, plus free exchanges after that.

How exhilarating it used to be to schedule dates with him! He'd say, "If I were being forward, I'd ask you to fondue, I'd ask you to come back to my place with me." These days he doesn't have to ask. We're already both at home, we're already on a date. To be married is to be on a perpetual date. A nightmare date that runs the whole course of your life.

My husband laughs when I say this. His mother, when he repeats it, not so much. Villas yes, laughter no. Imagine her shock when we were introduced. What happened to the vetted woman, the daughter of a friend, who'd bought links for his French cuffs? I was nervous. So was my husband. "Don't worry," he said in the elevator, which to my great surprise glided straight to the foyer of his childhood home. My mother-in-law was just beyond the sliding doors, and I offered her my hand. "Nice to meet you," I said. I was afraid to touch the furniture, afraid to break a vase. She sat at the opposite end of the couch, as if I were contagious, and poured coffee into souvenir cups. My husband shoveled words into the silence. I ate all the cookies on the plate. We went on for months like this. Sipping coffee. Breaking the ice. One day my mother-in-law decided she had no choice but to give in. No more cookies. We switched to tea. After that, it was as if she'd chosen me herself.

The morning after Herod, I woke up early, feeling strange. My husband was still asleep, dreaming postcoital dreams. After watching him for a time I went into the kitchen and found the bottle of wine we'd shared. The ashtrays we had filled. The stars had been so crisp and clear, unlike anything we see living in the city, and now the sky was gray. On the porch, I pulled on the bra from the day before. The air was cool and the bird's wings spread wide under the eaves, its feathers laced with frost. Poor little bird. It had died so carelessly.

That morning I jogged long. I began on the same route I'd run every morning since we arrived. Down the path, past the log pile and the little pond where the land began to slope. It was too early even for the Germans or the Milanese; the landscape was all for me. It emptied onto the horizon. The dry grass. The delicate frost. For so long I had imagined the landscapes rendered by da Vinci to be mere fantasies of Tuscany; the soft edges in *The Virgin and Child*, the one with Saint Anne, belonged to a whole world made of butter. But as it turned out there are hours of a Tuscan day when this is exactly the case, when the light slides just so across the hills. The trees. The cypresses blur, evaporating. I ran through a row of them, along a ridge, past the villa nearest ours. I came to the point where normally I turned around and then ran farther still. Tractors tore through the painted silence. I met a hill. It was so steep I slowed to a walk. I thought of pilgrimages on which devotees climb stone steps on their knees to kiss a statue's feet. Here I was working through my own penance in the dust. For what? I gave up. Or my legs gave up. I stopped. Before me was a clearing, and in the clearing, a church. The door was open, expectant.

It was cool and bare and very quiet inside. My sneakers felt uncanny on the stone—I had half a mind to take them off. I found the plaque by the pews. This was a tenth-century church, I read, that had burned down twice. I placed a palm against the wall. Cool as cellar fruit. A votive candle flickered at the altar. The flame was new and the wick burned tall, though it struck me no one had been inside in quite some time. There was nothing in the donation box; no coins rattled when I tapped the side. I looked around. There were no deacons, no guards, no ticket takers peddling plastic rosaries and souvenirs. The church was empty save its cross, candles, plaque, and pews, and I was very alone. I approached the altar. I slipped a second candle from its pigeonhole and tipped the wick to the eternal light. For whom? For whom should I light this candle? I paused. The wax dripped, sealing the epistle of my thumb. I settled the flame into its stand. Then I stood in the door and looked into the shadows of the apse. How pure it must have felt in these small stone rooms, in those centuries when people still believed. And it was this idea, maybe, that compelled me to kneel on the stone. The candle flickered. I knelt until something in me announced it was time to go. Then I stood up and jogged away. When I looked back, the church had disappeared behind an unmarked crest. I felt the beauty of my secret—it was mine alone. And yet, as I neared the villa, I was filled with a desire to share what had happened to me. I felt the need to show my husband, to bring him to that hill and have him see what I had seen. It was only as I came up the path, past the pond, past the newly wakened Germans in their trekking gear, that I realized visiting the church with someone else wouldn't work. Two would ruin everything. Still, I felt the great desire to confess. It came upon me with the same urgency one feels, in winter, to stamp a foot into fresh snow. The truth was this: I could be a tourist, or I could be alone.

I slowed to a walk. The dirt gave way to grass. I rounded the corner of the villa. There was my husband, on his knees, the earth before him textured by a grave. He smoothed it with a trowel. I stood very still, watching the sun in his hair. It hadn't occurred to me, while I was gone, that he might be holding a vigil of his own.

Sometimes I miss those early months of courtship, when everything was still uncertain. Those days when we still lived apart—it was only a year ago. It seems to me there is something lost to those hour-long train rides. The thrill of the ask. The space. One gets so used to one's routines, living on one's own. Towel turbans, pajamas on the chair. Noodles over the sink. My question is, How to live alone, together, without living a lie? I knew a poet once who thought of an elegant solution. When her lover asked her to marry him, she said that perhaps he ought to rent the apartment across the hall. In the future I will never marry unless we agree to live apart. But close by. Not that I'll ever have the chance. I know I'm lucky to have a husband like mine.

From time to time I take out the postcard print that I brought back from Tuscany, my only nonedible souvenir. It is a postcard I will never send. I examine it at night, in the damask dim of the kitchen, over a clandestine cigarette. I read the back: *Annunciation with Saint Margaret and Saint Ansanus*, by Simone Martini and Lippo Memmi (1333). I trace the outline of Mary's disdain. How royal she looks. I sit with her in the kitchen, on the maroon chess-board of the tiles. I think, sometimes, how different things would be if only she'd kept the whole thing to herself. I wonder which way the world would tilt. And what if she'd said no?

SIBERIA

"I have no pictures of people on my phone anymore," she said, "only pictures of prose. When did I become a misanthrope?"

The last time he saw her, she wore the same dress she'd worn the day the affair began. He thought of that dress. She thought of the hurt. No pictures of either, really.

She had to scroll back quite some ways to find faces. They made their first (last) appearance circa that last time they'd spoken. So this was a clue. Before that, people. After, novels, chrysanthemums, butterflies, an opera box. Here was a scene in which an off-duty actor slaps the proprietor with a lavender glove . . . She read the first bit aloud, then trailed off. A whole year's worth. So that's what she'd been up to. What did it say, this careful collection of nonhumanoid excerpts— "An increased chance of dying alone," he joked.

On her end, the sirens began to sound.

The general consensus regarding the conflict raging outside was this: someone would win. Then life would return to the way it was before. A very few would have quite a lot, a very many not much at all. The civilian population stayed in and waited for the insurgents and the government to sort it out, i.e., they did as they were told. Meanwhile they logged in. Logged on. Looked into their screens. Unwrapped food rations marked with insurgent symbols in districts the insurgents controlled, government insignias in the government zones. They stood at the windows, a safe step back from the panes, and watched the drones and searchlights spar. They sat in stairwells and called old lovers they'd formerly sworn off.

Because life had slowed down enough for almost everything to be forgiven. The subway was empty. The restaurants, closed. The streets were quieter than they'd ever been, people said again and again; on an unsecured line it was hard to come up with anything else to talk about. For a while, between the hours of noon to five, you could still walk down the block to the salon for powdered shampoo and razors, where they were also selling cigarettes. Then the hours of free movement slendered down to a thin band of light and disappeared: perpetual night. There was no such thing as curfew anymore. It was all the time. The risk of either asking to see the other, rekindle the relationship, had been thus eliminated. In other ways, life hadn't changed. For her, for him. She was a playwright. He was a playwright. The theaters were always the first thing to go.

She said, "Maybe we should write some monologues."

He was on speakerphone as she scrolled. The stairwell was alive with the afterfizz of disinfectant. She sat at the top, tucked up under the roof, twirling the end of her braid between forefinger and thumb. She wondered if he did other things while they talked, absentminded tasks like cleaning the counter, stewing a chicken, making soup. One could harmonize with these distractions. They were intimate chores to be completed in the presence of someone you love. When she heard the clack of the keyboard, her heart sank. As for typing emails, transcripts, refreshing the news—these tasks were discordant with reconciliation. She might as well hang up.

For his part, he didn't imagine her to be doing anything at all, because he knew exactly where she was. She'd observed the stairwell in great detail for him, down to the convex skylight overhead. He could picture her, and accurately: spotlit, linoleum, slumped.

Her face, propped against the railing, was obscured by a stiff veil of unwashed fringe. The bangs quivered in the gust of a door collapsing on a pressurized hinge, the narrowing gap resisting until that last moment when—

"I think this building used to be a school," she said.

What he'd loved about the woman was this space she left between what she said and what she meant. He liked a buffer zone. Standing in his kitchen, polishing the steel countertop while the kettle rumbled on the burner, prepping a cup of tea he already regretted and did not want, he pressed the phone to his ear and reflected that this quality reproduced in her the same power of a play: you sat safely back from the struggles on stage. He didn't see so many plays anymore, of course. Nobody did. These days, he mostly watched YouTube clips of classical musicians. He chose a passage—the cello ascension, say, the grand stairwell entrance, to the center of Bach's Suites—and watched many cellists attempt it, one after the next. He ranked them on a Post-it secured to his desk.

And he watched her. In his mind. That dress she used to wear was of a high blue color with long tight sleeves, the kind of conservative garment that nevertheless immediately called to mind how difficult it must be to get on or, more to the point, off. He'd appreciated that. He ripped open a package of tea. ("What's that sound?" she asked. "My latest vice," he replied; before the curfew he'd collected quite a stash.) He sometimes wondered if they'd made a mistake, separating themselves. Though it was hard to say what was a mistake, what wasn't, when everything ended in disappointment anyway. That's how he'd wound up with so much tea, really—you get sick of a flavor and abandon the box. This was his belief. So it was more about how much time they might have spent but hadn't. He steeped his unwanted—he checked the label—Darjeeling. Terrible substitute for nicotine. It was terrible to quit. He wondered what even was the point of soldiering on. Out the window, the searchlights sliced through each other, illuminating the slats of fire escapes. He could see a shadowed figure across the way, another shape in the yellow light, someone also making tea, thinking, reverse engineering how they might have lived. The age gap between him and the woman on the line stretched nearly twenty years. She was too young to remember the last time war broke out.

He drew the frilled demi-curtain along the rod. The apartment was full of ironic feminine kitsch like this. Cotton eyelet in the kitchen; a hip-high vase at the door. There were antique advertisements for nylons, framed, in the bath, details that seemed at once an appeal to the fairer sex and also a light joke at his exes' expense: after they left, domestic life went on.

The stair landing in which the woman sat, meanwhile, or so she was now saying, was a revolving furniture exchange—one of the computer chairs had once belonged to her. The purpose was stated right there on the wall with a little handmade sign: CAROUSEL OF EXCHANGE. And yet, despite the sundry furnishings, she sat on the floor, on the top step. It was neatly done, the way the man had staged it in his mind, and not so far from the truth, as he and the woman would both have been pleased to know. It is a fantasy too often underappreciated, being guessed at correctly through the presumption of stage directions:

[*Spotlight. Woman seated at edge of stage, feet dangling into orchestra pit to simulate stairs; alternatively, elevated, stage left, visible railing, against which she rests head. Presses phone to ear. Secondhand furniture scattered. Lots of it. Broken chairs. A real junkyard. Possibly a candlestick.*]

[*Woman touches her hair. Stands up. Looks out the barred window and spins a chair.*]

SHE: Do you know that story, the one with the toboggan and the two kids, the boy and the girl, and he takes her every day to the top of a hill, it's snowing, and they sled down three times, one, two, three, they're at some dacha somewhere, I think it's Chekhov—one sec, I have it on my phone, or never mind, it takes too long to find—anyway, he's sitting behind her, arms around her, and each time they descend, he whispers in her ear, I love you, Nadya, just quietly enough that she can't be sure she heard it, and at the bottom of the hill, when she asks him what he said, he says, What are you even talking about, so she lets him drag her back to the top, even though she hates sledding, she's terrified, the hill is too steep, because the whole time she's trying to decide, Was it him, or was it the wind?

[*Beat.*]

HE: The rule of threes, I know it, sure. But at least I never dragged you up hills.

She sat back down on the stairs, returned to scrolling through the collection of passages on her phone. Her face was blanched by the screen, the walls by the light pollution burned off in the night to settle, like ash, through the skylight. She slid back up to the passage with the lavender glove.

SHE: It's the lavender that makes it Nabokov's. A compromise between the slapstick and the lovely.

[*Beat.*]

SHE: The problem is I have no audience for these observations.

[*Stage right, man takes cloth and mimes polishing a countertop, stops. Examines his hand.*]

SHE: I guess what I'm trying to say is that I've been thinking lately about whether I should have gone in for women.

HE: Well, I'm definitely the right audience for that.

Outside, the sirens sounded again.

Maybe all drama reduces to a siren's call: there's something in a person that craves catastrophe. The little ticket-taker in everyone longs for hiatus, release, the distant crash of buildings tumbling down, perhaps even not so distant, just far enough away to still keep safe while last century's rubble is pulped. The slow disaster unfolding outside whets the appetite for more. Six of one, half dozen. (Between two tyrants, it's tempting to choose the one who's not yet let you down.) A last push against the door of the imagination, and then it is ajar, revealing scenes beyond the current desertion of the streets: your own building, halved, the small world of your room revealed to the no one left who's looking in. Squint into the sun. There, the end. You don't admit thoughts like these. You catch them reflected in the periphery, in the opera glasses glinting in the darkened mezzanine. *Not political enough, Nadya* ... The weird echo arrives, escaped from a pamphlet, a newspaper, something else she's read— But no, it's just the hiss and crash of the pressurized door in the stairwell again.

The real reason she'd called was to discuss the question of loyalty. There was a war on. One was naturally preoccupied with taking sides. And yet she found she still wanted to please, primarily, this person on the other end of the line. She'd played many roles over the years, never quite able to shake the sense that she was in fact performing for someone offstage, and that her life was therefore misdirected. This audience was present even in her most private moments, observing what she ordered on a dinner date, what she did in bed. It watched her pin up bits of dialogue on note cards to organize her thoughts. There was some satisfaction, at least, in thinking that perhaps she'd made of him a muse. Not everyone found one. So that was their loss. The world had been wrung of ancientness, made practical, was too afraid of running into itself to indulge in clichés like these.

SHE (*to the audience, whispering*): He always did have a special way of making me feel ashamed.

HE: What?

SHE: Nothing, nothing.

NEIGHBOR 1 (*stage left, lowering pair of binoculars, sinking behind tin trash can*): I think they're finally losing it.

Down three flights of stairs, the building accordioned per city regulation, the façade jutting in and out, stepwise, to maximize access to light. Across the niche from the woman's apartment, her neighbors liked to keep track of her progress: she studied her note cards, pasted papers to the wall. They observed one another brushing their teeth, painting toenails, steeping the coffee, and dressing for work. There was no need to dress for work or maintain pedicures, but they half dressed all the same, made the coffee, filed the corns. The neighbors couldn't have known the woman was writing plays, of course. That was part of the intrigue. Tit for tat: she watched them too. What did they do, for example, in that apartment two floors above, where they always kept the red light on? Where did one even find such lightbulbs? She'd looked it up once: *bulb red free shipping District 31.* The couple was cooped up in the ruby light right now, looking through the reddish pall to the woman's empty studio.

Where could she possibly have gone?

To the stairs, that's where, and where she was still trying to train her thoughts on logically compatible conclusions. She glanced around her at the walls of the former school. She hadn't spent much time on this landing before, had visited only once or twice, when she'd had a guest and needed an extra seat, or else had an extra seat (that abominable computer chair, for example, which bucked and squeaked) of which she had need to dispose. She imagined children running up these stairs, trying to make it to class, trying to make out. At that moment, it struck her as far more likely that the building had debuted as a hospital or an asylum. She rested her forehead on the rail, picked at the hard denim seam that ran the length of her jeans. There was a demon in her, she thought. Some flutter in her mind suggested itself, and what it whispered was: *Don't be foolish, Nadya, and take what you can get . . .*

On the other end of the line, the man was thinking that she sounded very young, and lovely, lovely in a way that emphasized how young she was. He hoped she'd live a long time. He looked out his window to the empty street, where nostalgic municipal authorities had preserved the cobblestones. A figure darted across them, stumbled, fell. The spotlights rounded the corner after it.

HE: Look out your window. Look out your window and tell me what you see.

The two found themselves watching similar scenes on different sections of the same street. The searchlights hawked revenge on sidewalks, swept shadows for loose change. The conversation slowed to an exchange of breath. Her building was on the corner, she could see two streets at once, where a different figure darted, disappeared, took cover in the hooded entrance of a former grocery store. The man enjoyed a midblock perspective, from which he watched a broken shape struggle to stand on the stones without drawing further attention to itself. The woman rose on tiptoes to peer through the barred window in the stairs. Her view was empty again. On the other end of the line, the man cradled cold tea to his chest. A spill stained his collar when the shot arrived. Not that she could have known.

SHE: They've put up propaganda over all the store signs, "We protect you" and the like. Do you have those?

HE: I honestly don't know.

He watched the slow shine spread around the fallen figure, a diadem for the head.

NABOKOV: If a butterfly appears on the wall in Act One—

CHEKHOV: —then its wings should ignite in Act Two.

[*Burst of sapphire from stage left. Beat.*]

NEIGHBOR 2: Shit role that guy got.

NEIGHBOR 1 (*cleaning binocular lenses with a cloth*): I auditioned for the lead, do you think that maybe—?

NEIGHBOR 3 (*sinking behind tin trash can*): I confess to a creeping sense of desperation.

(BECKETT (*offstage*): Leave me out of this.)

The following week they were back on the stairs, back on the phone. The insurgents had either seized or liberated nearby District 36, depending on your perspective, and to celebrate had let everyone out for a time. Or so her news sources said. The government districts, they figured, would now have to respond in kind. They were like the kids of divorced parents who compete for affection.

SHE: It says here for an hour, maybe even more—

HE: I'll come see you.

SHE: We'll meet halfway.

The faint gong of his forehead as it fell against the glass.

HE: What I wouldn't do, you know, to get outside today.

The woman confessed that some afternoons, in even the most anemic sun, she went up to the roof. She had a row of cacti up there, she explained, shriveled and frozen in little terracotta pots. Did he think they'd grow back? He didn't answer for a long time. "I'm not sure that's safe," he said. "I bet you could nearly see me if you stood on yours," she replied. Soft tan lines had set up camp on her shoulders, earned despite the chill. She suggested them, and he bronzed the image in. It was fine, she argued. They weren't *so* strict during daylight. He felt angry with her anyway for risking it, even as he admired the freckles beneath her eyes. He didn't want to seem overprotective, too concerned, so he changed the subject. The large desk where he sat was topped with glass, so that it offered a faint reflection. Google Maps filled his screen edge to edge.

He told her how *he'd* been traveling, lately. He tracked people around the world, checked the restaurant ratings, reviews of parks and libraries and bureaucratic offices, of galleries, cafés, and museums. Recently, he'd been in the habit of reading hospital recommendations and trailing patients across Russia. The reviews were translated automatically. Sometimes the same patient had visited multiple hospitals, seeking second opinions on chances of survival. He liked these recurring characters; they were his friends. He admired their will to live. He asked her if she was at her computer now and then remembered that, no, of course not, she was in the stairwell, where he'd left her. "But when you are," he said, and gave her the name of some province.

HE: They translate automatically, so you just find a hospital, and then, well, here's one. "Waited four hours, no bribes." That's not so bad, actually, compared to what I've seen in rural areas. But there's this one woman, let me find her, here, I think she has some problem with her stomach, she's been to at least nine clinics in the area. And by area, I mean a huge fucking swath of Siberia.

SHE: Maybe she's a hypochondriac.

The woman peered through the bars at the propaganda that had rebilled the old stores across the street.

SHE: Or maybe she's dying and doesn't want to believe it.

HE: "Very nice hospital. Train staff with dialogue to show listening to patients. You constantly have to wait even for payment through the cashier, the cashier was waited for two hours."

SHE (*laughing*): It's a relief to me, you know, that the algorithms are still shit.

HE: "In the ambulance, you can turn the clock around."

She navigated to her own maps. Her battery sounded its tinny alarm. She chose a town at random, not the one he had suggested, swiped away the notification that the device would soon be dead. There: a frozen place, high definition. Trees bent deeply over the road, knighted by snow. A tent in the woods was choked up by a stovepipe and its stream of smoke. Ice sculptures were dyed bright colors, the way the woman used to when she was just a girl and in the habit of shaping the snowfall into igloos. Her mother mixed the dye in spray bottles once filled with cleaning supplies, which the girl, now the woman, used to inflict garish patterns on the yard. The sculptures on the screen were arranged beneath a string of flags made ragged by the wind.

SHE: Do you think it's better, over there?

NABOKOV: Ha!

NEIGHBOR 1 (*raising then lowering binoculars*): Depends on your perspective.

She carried the phone down the stairs, through the pressurized door, down the hall, cupping the speaker to her chest. Went to open her door, found it was unlocked again. "That's not smart; please, take care of yourself." "I know, I know," she said. "One sec." Inside, she connected jack to cord. Slipped off her shoes by the bed. "Why do you sound like you're inside a Trojan horse?" "Just my apartment, you're on speaker." She turned on the lamp. "One sec again, the people across from me like to stare." "Get curtains," he said. "I have a curtain," she replied, sliding a piece of newspaper, slipped onto the rod by loops of string, across the pane. "Do you want some tea?" "Sure, I fucked mine up." "Okay, I'll get it. You play some music," she said.

He was still at his desk, in front of the maps. Outside, a cleanup crew bustled. Michelin men in white bodysuits pointed fine hoses at the cobblestones, where last week's stains remained. He thought about splicing in this elision now, narrating the shot to her as if it were occurring at this moment, right now, because it felt wrong to have witnessed it alone, to be forever distracting her with things like hospital reviews in O— province. His laptop was an oyster open to the world. Escape was always almost possible. The brash light of the screen brought out the gray in his face. The tabs were open to ice storms, mountains decadent with snow, a hospital lobby, movie clips, a streaming app on which he borrowed music, incognito. He loaded the clip of the cellist and pressed play, held the phone close to his ear to catch the sound of the woman moving through her little room. He imagined those sheer, breathy curtains, floor-length, that young women like, as if they all aspire to live inside a lung. Or maybe she'd simply tacked up a sheet. He couldn't remember how long she'd lived in this room. The addresses forsook him, washed away in the current of recent silence. He couldn't remember if this was the room he'd visited a few years ago, when her life had seemed so upsettingly haphazard. Perched on a wooden chair taken from the stairwell, for free, he'd felt that he had something to do with the observable impermanence. She used to become abstracted sometimes in very hot weather, most often after sex. She'd even faint. Crouched there on the bathroom tiles, holding her as she came to, he'd considered the weight of the soul. He felt a pang now, felt the pull of the white suits outside. Her voice drew him sharply from his reverie.

SHE: This is depressing.

HE: I thought that was my charm.

[*Muzak or satellite radio jazz audible from offstage.*]

SHE: No, the music. It's depressing. Play something else.

[*Beat.*]

HE: They're cleaning up over here. Or they were cleaning up.

SHE: Oh.

HE: They're gone now. It's fine. Please be more careful.

SHE: Okay.

HE: It's real.

[*Beat.*]

SHE: They're brave, you have to give them that. I wish I believed in something half as much.

HE: Yes, there's that.

[*Man leans against imaginary window again, peers down.*]

HE: All the same, I'm glad you don't.

The neighbors across from the woman's apartment were intrigued to see her light was on. Sympathizer, they guessed. She fit the insurgent type. Young. Idealistic. Putting up quotes all over the walls. Not nearly afraid enough. And one of the only other human beings in range, really, to develop theories about.

They watched her shadow flicker through the paper shade. (She was on to them, they were on to each other, the whole air shaft fluttered with headlines meant to keep out peeping Toms and Janes.) The paper fit imperfectly over the window, and when she crossed the room, it was possible to catch glimpses through the gaps. She wore a red sweatshirt and blue jeans. Her hair was down, kinked from a braid. The couple with the red bulbs watched her draw it up into a knot. Phone wedged between cheek and shoulder, she pulled the newspaper back an inch herself and peered out. One floor below, a man was looking back: one of his hands was pocketed, the other held a beer. She raised her eyes a floor above, to see what was happening up there.

The neighbors had never been the type to draw much attention to themselves. That's why she'd stayed. She waited tables at the trattoria around the corner—or had—and then came home to fix her plays. They were all of them in this building quiet by nature and hourly waged. No one meant to pry. At the moment there was simply nothing else to do. Sometimes a bird dove through the brick channel between the windows, and they envied it. They craned their necks, considered that *someone* had had the job of designing the tower on which those searchlights stood. The beer fizzed, the red light bled its liquid glow and rinsed the thought away. They thought of the sea, the way the sea-foam mouthed off onto the shore. The whole block cupped an ear to catch the sound of waves. One missed the beach. Another missed the women.

NEIGHBOR 1: What I wouldn't do for a proper steak—

NEIGHBOR 2: —or a long drive—

NEIGHBOR 3: —or an unskunked beer—

NABOKOV: The devil is in the details, and all great stories are fairy tales.

NEIGHBOR 3: I'll show you where the fucking fairies are—

NABOKOV: The gardener used naphthalene, my mother the ether, and I myself later used many killing agents. I looked forward to the crunch of a pin going through the chitinous thorax—

NEIGHBOR 2 (*rolling eyes, then lifting binoculars to them*): Right, so that was the difference between them.

The woman carried her teacup to the bathtub, ran a bath. He sat at his desk with his cold chamomile, imagining hers fresh. They listened to the water run.

For a brief period during which his wife, now ex, had been abroad, perhaps pursuing an affair of her own, the woman on the phone had stayed with him for an extended time. He had an image of her, perched on the rim of the tub, watching him shave.

They worked in the same room, she with her note cards, he with his YouTubes and Bach and half-hearted drafts. He was able to forget about her, he found, only when she was here, both of them engaged. For her it must have been the same. He was introduced to her absentmindedness—in particular, her absentmindedness of him—a side to her he'd not witnessed before. He observed the automatic gesture with which she tied her robe when she exited the bed, hours after sex, loose and unembarrassed. At noon she boiled eggs. The peeled shells plinked in the sink basin. She let the cooking water cool and collected it in a beaker for watering the plants. Feminine touches, the both of them. His, the anemic fern; hers, watering it with calcified runoff in which she'd boiled eggs. And this had frightened him greatly, noticing how easily she slipped into a routine. It was this, the saving of the water for the fern, that had broken him. He grew cagey, avoided sex, stood in the kitchen and raised his eyebrows at whatever she said, scratching the nape of his neck. "Okay," she said. "I understand." And left. He missed her immediately. It was there, a drug laced round the edges of his relief. More potent than he wanted to admit. When his wife returned, he was confused. Her body felt unfamiliar beneath his hands. "What's for dinner?" she asked. Anything but eggs.

The woman on the phone, whom he maybe still missed, was meanwhile theorizing about him. "It's involuntary," she was saying. She was perched on the edge of her own tub, nursing her mug and the phone. Nursing old wounds: "It's almost as if you think too fast," she said, "like you scheme without helping it." "Gee, thanks." "I only mean, it's like your schemes come to you all at once, impulses complete, so it's not like they're premeditated." "I'll take that as a compliment," he said. "I'm just saying," she added, "I don't think it's intentionally manipulative." "Has it ever occurred to you that you're pretty manipulative yourself?" "I never said I wasn't."

"But you implied by comparison." "I don't think it's always preferable," she said, "to think things all the way through to the consequences." "Like not calling for a year?"

SHE: Funny, in my books, it's you who didn't call me.

The woman drew her lower lip between her teeth. The newspaper that hung over the window fluttered. It was the flight of juvenility, she thought, fluttering through the door. She sank a hand into the bath to test the temperature. It came out scalded, red to the wrist.

"It's been a shitty year," she said.

She taught him foreign idioms. She explained how to beat an egg white in French, *monter en neige*, and with what tool, in German, i.e., a *Schneebesen*. In every other language, she noted, to beat an egg white means make snow, whereas— "We're using the short end of the stick," he joked. The insurgents had gained further territory and were letting all their subjects out. Permanently. For good. They were closing in; they were winning; they would be here soon. The man and the woman could not resist the contagion of the festive mood. She laughed. She was ready, she said. Even overprepared. When not on the phone, she often sat in the tub for hours, listening to language courses. Her legs were covered in razor nicks incurred while conjugating irregular verbs and gendering the nouns: *der, die, das*. She spoke a little of everything by now. That was company, she thought. A bit of static interference and civil-sounding chatter she couldn't understand. She rotated through, disc-jockeying German, Hindi, Russian, French. She was fit to renounce her language for the native tongue of the invaders, the liberators, ha ha, whoever it was that came next. She knew how to thank them, how to curse them, how to plead: no rape.

HE: Do you still have that dress?

The man on the phone had an excellent tub, one of those claw-footed basins that swallows you whole. She'd long had the goal of bathing in it. In those intervals when he was not already engaged, or married, or monogamous, they'd gone instead to the public baths. The memory made her smile, though it also dredged up pain. In the swell of steam, the full force of him had been delegated to the blurry shapes of other people. She remembered she'd worn a leotard, self-conscious about her figure, but you could hardly see anyone in here, she could have worn nothing at all. The Lycra clung to her belly like a blister. What a relief afterward to step out into the cold. And how superior the sex, later that night, in bed. Her body felt purged and compact, a polished seed. That was the way of the saunas in the public baths. You waited, you suffered, and when the suffering lifted—

SHE: I used to think you should have given me your place when you were away. You have all that space! Me, I open the oven and sit down on the bed.

HE: Come on over.

SHE: Thank you.

HE: Only I'm sick of it, I'd rather take you somewhere else.

SHE: Where then?

HE: I'd think that was obvious.

She tapped a foot to the surface of the water, still scalding. The bathroom swirled with steam. She breathed in deep and choked. A drip of sweat ran down her chin. She cracked open the door. Closed it again. Then, like an afterthought, she swung it wide. There was nothing better than a hot bath in winter chill! But she had just the one window, where her neighbors kept watch. That was her one request, she said, wherever they went: a magnificent tub and a cool cross-breeze. She would have liked to open everything, lift the windows and unlock the doors. It was a game of chicken, she thought. That was life. Who would draw the curtains first? She was tired of waiting, tired of accommodating. Of simply delaying capitulation, and the sordid pleasure that came with it. The suspense, she supposed, was in the when, the how much, you inevitably gave. She stood from the bath and crossed the room. The towel slipped. Delirious, ecstatic, she wedged the phone between cheek and shoulder, wedged her hands under the lip of the window, struggling to raise the pane. She told him to hold on, one sec, I just— She braced a foot against the sill, pushed with the strength of her legs. The window gave and welcomed in the cold. The release drew her up to her full height, into the top pane, so that for a moment she stood like a stained-glass saint stuck in the window of a church. Then the bullet came in and opened up her chest. She was reminded that, at geological depths, the earth seethes with something like wrath.

He stared perplexed at the phone in his hand. "One sec," she'd said. He checked the screen again to make sure she hadn't hung up.

Crossing the apartment to the bath, he flipped on the switch.

"Hello?"

There was the tub, gleaming beneath the showerhead. The framed nylons ad, in which a model rolled the shadow of a stocking up her shin. He imagined the woman instead. She was seated on the rim with her tea, in a towel, her thighs extended from the hem. She'd become extremely heavy when she fainted, he recalled. He'd press a cold washcloth to her wrists. He was good at waiting. He looked at the phone. Leaving the light on, he returned to his desk. He stared into the laptop screen at the brutalized hospitals and lands exposed to permafrost, now not so permanent. They were all awaiting miracles, these isolated towns. They willed a change in the tilt of the earth, the melting of the straits. Soon enough, the ships would sail through, like blood back into a resuscitated heart. And so they clung.

His own reflection flashed in the window. He'd gained weight, lost hair, this past year. She'd be disappointed to see him when she did. The phone was still pressed to his ear. He used to fantasize about fucking her in public restrooms, at parties, in other people's kitchens; it would be such a relief to be caught, to confess. He swiveled in his chair and looked back into the soft white glow of the empty bath, the gleam of the tiles faint. He recalled the way she flinched, and violently, if he so much as touched a fingertip to the vertebrae of her neck. What he'd like to do is take her to the Russian baths, had they done that yet? He'd like to take her halfway around the world, up north, away from everyone they knew, their prying gaze, buy a plot of land and wait for the earth to thaw. A shadow shifts, something flickers in the bath. He listens, waiting for her to catch her breath, finish her sentence, call him back. Obviously they'll learn, they'll speak whatever she likes, he'll tell her everything she's ever wanted to know in as many languages as he can manage, *Schnee* and *neige*, and when the time comes, should it ever come to that, he'll talk her softly into death. The silence stretches on, indifferent as a government—but you know all about that.

WEIMAR WHORE

She'd bought ten kilos bulk, the calculation being that it would keep her alive at the lowest cost. (Imagine the trouble though, carrying it back.) Look at her now. On hands and knees with the dustpan and a boar bristle brush, sweeping it all up. Pure gold! Rice never devalues itself. Mostly she was sending further grains to their final resting places beneath the floor while her boarder looked on from the hall. He cut a pensive picture there, one arm braced against the jamb.

"It's 2021," he said, deep in thought. "Why are you acting like some Weimar . . . ?"

He trailed off, because harsh words don't need repeating. They stay said. She heard them still. Curled over the dustpan, she cocked her head into his ellipsis. Rob! The friend of a friend whose finances were such that he needed a place to stay for a while. Inconveniently named the same as her ex. (Was that why she'd taken him on?) She turned back to the rice.

"You could help, you know."

Rob had a point. Our heroine had undeniably adopted certain Weimar habits. Taking in boarders. Fretting over inflation. Stewing cabbages while darning her socks. (And if Rob was lucky, his socks, too.) The truth was she'd overdosed on the media of the interwar period. She couldn't keep both feet in the now. It had all started with the other Rob—romantic Rob—the historian whom she hadn't seen in weeks, and whom she therefore now thought of as Rob the Ex. It was from him that she'd picked up the tendency to conflate eras, her fascination with fashionably degenerate times. His sudden departure had only hastened her decline.

Meanwhile: "It's a bit!" she said, in total denial with a friend on a walk along the *Bahn* tracks. "You can be the eighties, ha ha." She popped a heel onto the low stone wall to ratchet the laces up the tedious hooks of her ankle boots. The friend waited at the chicken wire fence. "Which eighties?" she said. Across the tracks, anti-American graffiti splashed over the retainer wall. That war, too, was still going on.

"Maybe you'll slip further and further into the past," the friend continued. "Like to Prussia. Or the Napoleonic Wars. Maybe it turns out you're Polish . . ." She screwed up her face as if working through a long division problem.

The Weimar Queen wiped her palms on her long wool skirt. It was eighty-seven degrees. The friend was wearing shorts.

"Right, that's funny! What a hoot!" But it didn't work like that, our period piece knew. Not for her. She was a one-trick pony, temporally stationary, one might even say stuck, wholly tethered to the media she'd gorged. The world had moved on. In fact it was spinning farther out of reach, like a top on a string, farther and farther, until one day the string would give up and snap.

"Shit," she said, coming away from her boot with half a shoelace in her hand. Her thoughts whipped to the problem of string rations.

There is comfort in finding out that you're not the only one. In having your reality confirmed by two, or three, or any multiple at all. Though I suppose this is also what we call contagion. The psychiatrist, at least, was pretty sure he'd heard of other cases of the girl's condition. "I'm certain you're not the only Weimar . . ." His voice was low and strong. (While many people underestimate the psychiatric importance of a soothing vocal timbre, they should not.) The patient on the chaise sighed so heavily into her wool she seemed to shrink. A knee sock slumped down her knee with visible relief.

He asked her to describe her symptoms once more.

"I feel like an inflation crisis," she said. Supine on the ratty chaise (and how many decades had *it* absorbed?), she pointed at her chest. There was a chaos in her heart and a numbness in her arms that she'd tried to treat by eating garlic. It was supposed to be good for you. But perhaps in her case contra . . . indicated. Her vocabulary was going too. A lot of outdated ideas had stowed away inside her head. Maybe they'd always been there. The point was, she couldn't stop heeding them. The present, pegged against these notions, steadily lost purchase. She wagged her stockinged feet. "I'm beginning to feel—" and here she whispered "—like it's everyone *else* who's nuts."

"Hm," said the psychiatrist, setting down his pen. "Can you say more about that?"

A man of his word, that night the psychiatrist gathered his case notes at his desk. It was his grandfather's desk, his grandfather's chaise; psychiatry was the family trade. A new ring seared itself into the old veneer as he steeped his tea; generations of Greenbergs had wreaked teapot tempests here. *Why go back? Who cares?* his grandfather had said when he announced plans to open a practice in Berlin. *Terrible country. I already moved the furniture once across the*

Atlantic ... The psychiatrist sighed. He pushed the old man out of his mind, straightened his spectacles, and returned to his case data.

There was a lot of it. Too much, in fact. That was part of the problem. The Weimar Queen had offered up her diaries. The idea was to locate just when, exactly, her affliction had begun. He eyed the stack of notebooks. There was something pathological simply in how prolific she'd been.

The entries started out normally enough—here was a first date with Rob the Historian—but by volume two the psychiatrist began to feel that the experiences recounted weren't the patient's at all. These were secondhand scenes, lifted from movies and novels a century old. He recognized the plagiarism only because, being something of a literary man himself, he had read the books in question. For example: a couple protested the Third Reich with a picture postcard campaign whose slogans had once been punishable by death but which now seemed fairly tepid. *The Führer is taking your sons! This is the cost of victory in France!* The difference in the patient's account was that she'd delivered the postcards herself. *Everyone's nice to you just before a death sentence*, she recalled. And as if that weren't already worrying enough, *Even the executioner.* That's how you knew they'd considered you an equal all along. It could have easily been them. But it had to be someone, and thus the entire courtyard was grateful for your service. In an entry dated only a few weeks before, the psychiatrist learned that it was a crime for firing squads to fire at the head. That's what the little red card pinned over the heart is for. *Here*, the attending doctor said, fastening the ace of diamonds to the silk pocket of the patient's best shirt. The psychiatrist turned the pages at random: a girl in rags walked the streets with a suitcase and a magnificent fur coat that, draped round the shoulders of a girl like her, was obviously stolen. How had no one noticed? Most things were borrowed, if you thought about it, the patient, now dabbling in socialism, suggested. One showed up at a friend's, offered to loan her a fur coat, and in return stayed until her husband came back from laying railroad tracks. Meanwhile, to be married oneself was to become vulnerable to heists: freedom, wages, all your friends. In a thumbtack magnate's suite, the patient ferreted three of the absent wife's red silk blouses into her own brassiere. The old fart, seated on the edge of the tub, didn't notice at all. *You know how it is*, she wrote, *they see what they want to see!* It was hardly in the industrialist's interest to reject a magically inflating bust. *And that's how the stock market crashed . . .*

The psychiatrist leaned back in his chair. He raised his arms and cracked his back. Outside, the street had softened to the post-commuter hush of night. The twin girls who lived across from him had hung up little glowing stars. He lit a cigarette. Smoke rose in pensive swirls. He studied the papers before him. Why dwell on such things? Why consciously resurrect a time when a raw egg yolk plus a dash of Worcestershire and schnapps could count as lunch? It had to be involuntary. Then again, everyone's pockets were becoming lighter by the hour. He could feel it himself. Invisible forces tugged at the lining of his pants. Supply had shrunk. Prices soared. Stubbing out the cigarette, he flipped a fat corner of volume four. He knew who his patients had been, what they'd done. That was his job. Less certain was the future. The question of what, under inflationary circumstances, they were capable of.

We've come to take your sons!

Across the city at the Weimar Queen's, all the lights were on. Three voices rose against each other. They carried into the *Innenhof*. Meanwhile, wakeful neighbors, sitting in kitchens in their nighties, drafted peevish, self-righteous notes to pin to the courtyard door.

You can probably guess the cause: the other Rob, the Historian and Ex, still in possession of a key, had made a surprise return. It was a real scene.

The Weimar Queen found herself in a translation pickle. One does wish the language in question were love. But it was just the usual barrier: Rob the Boarder *konnte kein Deutsch*. It was one of many reasons for the Historian to explode.

To his credit, Rob the Boarder was proving himself a clever man in other, nonlinguistic respects. Truth be told, he had indeed considered trying to date the Weimar girl, an amorous impulse of which he now stood accused. She had an apartment, after all. His current strategy was to deny. To appeal to the sympathies of his benefactress, he cowered into a corner of the sofa on which she'd so generously put him up. Standing strategically on the cushions, he clutched a throw pillow to his chest as he backed against the wall. It was a strong defensive position. "Oh!" he simpered as the jilted German bellowed. He was a peaceful man of creative ambitions. A little music, a little poetry; he dabbled here and there in documentary film, short clips collected on his phone in which many an unconsenting subject turned to the camera and said, in a language that despite six years in Neukölln Rob the Boarder still did not comprehend, *Shut that thing off you fucking twat or I will have your balls.* That's how everyone did documentary these days! It wasn't his fault if people didn't get it. They would soon enough, and then he'd be swimming in cash, part of which would go toward back-paying the present rent outstanding. "That's the problem!" he continued, the pillow spilling like stolen blouses over the corset of his arms. One didn't make much money following one's dreams. He despised the fetish for skilled immigrants. What about the skill of being sentient, of bearing witness, of simply being alive? What was it people had against the Australians anyway? Every human being was skilled simply by virtue of having survived. The immigration standard ought to be this: be sensitive and harmless. He raised a worker's fist. The Weimar Queen appeared to him saintlike, her hands pressed together as she pleaded for him to step down from the couch and lower his voice. The Ex, fuming and pacing on the other side of the room, took this opportunity to lunge. "I'm innocent, I'm innocent!" the cowering Boarder screamed. "I'm a lover not a fighter!" The Historian roared, "You are neither!" Then he clasped his hands over his ears, remembering he wasn't supposed to understand anything at all.

Back across the city, not a few blocks from the psychiatrist's, the language tutor was drinking in the bar he always visited after taking leave of the little heiresses he taught. He liked to sit here with a beer and a notebook at the end of a week, working up enough superiority to propel him home. He daydreamed. He jotted down some poems. Come last call, the bartender ignored his parting nod. Not to be deterred, the tutor saluted his imaginary audience and tottered out the door. The bus showed a fifteen-minute wait. He flashed the finger at the empty stop.

The tutor had earned the right to act out. The twins he taught every Tuesday and Thursday evening, for 80 percent of twice the price, could have hopped right out of the Brothers Grimm. And today, they'd fired him. "We don't want to learn German anymore," they'd said, in English, seated on matching velvet chairs with bows the size of kittens purring in their poufy hair. They had the oversized heads of children in storybooks, with the same problem that nothing much seemed to get in. *Hallo, hallo, habt ihr mich verstanden?* The girls giggled. He repeated himself. They giggled again. They swung their pudgy, stockinged legs. Tiny feet, stuffed into maryjanes, made good castanets of the furniture. *Girls*, their mother had so often cried from the other room, *cut that racket out!* You'd find them ten years from now in Zürich, still not speaking German, chattering away in untraceable international English while their father went on doing whatever he did (or didn't, depending on who was asking). The tutor rested his head against the S-Bahn window. Five more stops to Marzahn. Once home, he paused in the staircase leading up to his studio. Glanced across the well-illuminated *Hof*. Strange. This particular neighbor never left her lights on.

"Was hat er gesagt?!"

Rob the Historian and Ex, hands clapped firmly to either side of his head, demanded an explanation.

"You haven't visited here in weeks!" the Weimar Queen protested. What was she supposed to have thought? She'd taken on the Boarder to make ends meet and pay for the psychiatrist. It wasn't her fault that this Rob, too, was a dud.

"He says he's the peaceful, platonic type," she translated. "He really hasn't got anywhere else to go. And he hasn't got his *Aufenthaltsbewilligung*. Frankly—" and here she was not translating but extrapolating "—I don't think he'd survive. Let me show you." She steered Rob the Ex into the kitchen, where the potatoes she'd been peeling gleamed on the cutting board like Fabergé eggs awaiting filigree. She pointed to a mountain of bananas in the corner. "This is his idea of cooking," she said. Rob the Boarder had accepted an entire treeful of bananas at the food bank. A scattering of plastic sacks rustled across the floor. "You wouldn't believe how elated he was! I've eaten nothing but bananas for days," she told the Historian now. "I can't go on. What happens to a man like that when I put him on the street?"

"That's the thing! You aren't supposed to care! You're supposed to care about *me*! Besides, it's summer, it's not even cold. Why *are* you wearing wool?"

The other Rob cried from the sofa in the next room, "Have mercy!"

The Historian threw his hands up in disgust. "If *that's* what you want."

The language tutor, still in the stairwell, had often observed his thrifty neighbor. Her apartment was just opposite his, and she seemed not to believe especially in curtains. He'd seen her at the recycling, collecting bottles. Observed her modest décor. You could track her chintzy progress from room to room as the lamps flickered on and off. Not a volt wasted. Now there she was, every window ablaze, she herself glowing like the Siegessäule. How had he never noticed how beautiful she was? The radiance seemed to emanate directly from her skin. Alas, as always, he was too late. He could detect at least two male voices carrying across the courtyard, one very much in need of lessons.

The other neighbors, too, sensed an ending. They set aside their scrap papers and plots, their plans to report the Weimar girl to the relevant authorities, and shuffled back to bed, intuiting closure was nigh. The night grew still. Everyone quietly locked their doors. The two interloping Robs, one cowering on the sofa, the other at the door, were struck by the premonition that they had lingered too long. The lights flickered overhead. It occurred to the Ex that history shifts with the Will, the Spirit, the scepter, that revolutions descend like acts of grace, and that indeed such a transformation was taking place in the Weimar Queen at this very moment. And—ominous thought—he was directly within the blast radius. The potatoes she had been peeling when he arrived were ready ammunition. She loaded one up.

"You wait!" she cried. The grim prospect of her future—bananas, rice, vagrant gargoyles perched on her furniture, the endless potatoes with their larva glow—appeared to her all at once. The lost potential of her youth! It gave her power. It gathered around her in a neon haze and expended itself all at once. The Historian recognized it: the nimbus that hovers over all things just about to be destroyed.

"You wait right there," the Weimar Queen shouted down the hall. The Historian and Boyfriend—*now* finally the Ex?—had already placed a hand on the knob. "You chased *me*," she reminded him. "You showered me with superlatives until I gave in, even though I swore not to let anyone sink their hooks in. You *butcher*! You whore! Oh, you're moving in, you need a key, you need someone to edit your thesis. And then you fucking disappear? For weeks? Meanwhile I'm here taking care of strays. Mistakes were made, it's true. The past is the past. But quite frankly nothing is more offensive than your imagining that I would be attracted to *either of you*!" At this she cocked an arm and thrust the potato, shot put-style. It landed precisely at his sternum before dropping to the floor. A hint of fear rose in the Robs' eyes. "You absolute lemons!" The Weimar Queen's voice both rose and deepened, gaining the gravel of an operetta. "Both of you! *Raus! Raus!*" The thump of a broom handle from a last wakeful neighbor in the apartment above benchmarked just how loud she was. She chased Rob the Boarder around the sofa as he plucked his belongings from baseboards and lampshades and the backs of chairs. "What's happening?" he cried with a newly persecuted note. "What have you said?" No one answered, because truly only an idiot could have needed a translation.

The other Rob was prepared for his rival's ejection. Delighted, he held the door open as the professional drifter sprinted straight through and onto the stairs. He made to bolt the lock. "Oh no you don't," the Weimar Queen cried. "You too! Out! And take these bananas with you!" The rubbery skins bounced lifelessly as prosthetic limbs. Ducking, a hand thrown across his delicate face, the Historian took off. The fruit followed him down all four floors, splattering on the landings with big wet slaps. In the morning, the neighbors emerged. The whole staircase, booby-trapped.

What lies beneath a city? You could say rubble; you could say trash. Once upon a time the debris was piled and draped with dirt. Now we call them hills. Now we call them -bergs.

It may just as well be that the answer is debt. Unsteady foundations blown away in the quick breeze of an inflationary crisis. How light everything suddenly seems. That potato's about to float right out of your hand. In the metaphysics of the moment, the sublimation of your savings leaves you dizzy. What an ugly, unruly thing! The psychiatrist turned the page to a famous filmic ending: the undead are after revenge. Load the elevators. Seize the businessmen. The anticipation leaves a chill, a flutter in your chest, clutching at whatever you last held in your hands. The whole world rises and lifts away. The psychiatrist sighed, shut the notebook. He'd always been envious of the genius of his patients.

GETTYSBURG

"Anyway," their dining companion concluded, "to most people, this is more acceptable than that." She waved her fork on the diagonal, pointing first to her husband and herself, then to them. She and her husband were the this and they were the that. "Oh come on," she added, as if exasperated by their incomprehension. "Of course it matters which one of you is white." It was a very long dinner toward the end of an even longer year. After, they walked home along the river, just the two of them.

"I think we're becoming unsocialized."

"Yes, that must be it."

The advice, if that's what it was, was discarded from their minds, lightly as an empty tissue box. They didn't remember it until a few hundred miles into the road trip when, as is so often the case, you find yourself in need of tissues—he had just sloshed cold coffee across his lap ("Shit!")—and when, glancing out the window, you discover that you have no idea where you are. They'd spent the morning at Gettysburg. Now it was afternoon, and Jefferson Davis Highway unfurled seedily before them. Her uncle, an estranged relation getting on in years, lived somewhere off it; it was with him they'd spend the night. Meanwhile they ate up mile after mile with the amazement of people who've never driven this far south before.

"—a whole highway named after him!"

"—can you believe—!"

"*Go straight,*" directed the woman inside the phone, "*for two hundred kilometers.*" The road signs spoke miles, but Anand refused to trade the units he'd grown up with for a system demonstrably less sensible. He loaded up the playlist.

On the horizon, strong evidence of a storm.

"I thought we were too far inland for hurricanes."

"General apocalypse, I guess."

They took road trips like these once or twice a year. As the papers were fond of pointing out, many millions of millennials were reluctant to leave the coasts, had never even googled Yellowstone. And even if they did, or would, what they'd find was pictures of the thousands of foreign tourists who arrived by megabus each year to watch the geysers go.

So maybe the roadtrippers were entitled to feeling a bit superior. But they were still strangers in their own nation. Everyone is, if you drive far enough.

"But I *am* a foreigner."

"You just got citizenship. You're stuck with us now."

And what a big country it was! They'd taken the week to see some more. He'd autoreplied his .org inbox; she, her .edu. They'd filled the rental tank, stocked the cupholders with snacks, and taken off over the Verrazano. They didn't have to go so far before everything became unfamiliar. Really, just over the Verrazano. They rolled down the windows. The direction was south; the goal, Savannah. A Senate race was imminent, and they planned to knock on some doors.

Not until Jefferson Davis Highway did the dining companion's comment return. Diana was fishing through the plastic sacks for chips and further napkins.

"I wonder if we're not exactly the volunteer profile they're looking for?"

New York had the reach of cottonwood or pollen. It defined an ecosystem all its own. Only midway through Pennsylvania did you escape its sweep and a new kind of flora emerge: narrower roads; affordable real estate; tractor trailers galumphing down lane one. The Midwest loomed somewhere in Erie. You could tell by the way the land flattened and the woodlands narrowed to windbreaks between the farms, and by the layout of the convenience stores, which shared in common taupe wire shelves and the tart, musty smell of packaged bread. Onward to Ohio, where the interstates swung wide around modest skylines, giving the buildings wide berth, working up the centrifugal momentum to speed through Indiana, Illinois, on to someplace worth the hotel costs. Montana, maybe. Or Sun Valley, Idaho, where the vacation homes returned and the all-inclusive tour buses glided through bruised and violet landscapes as alien as advertised . . . That was last year's trip. On the way, they'd visited her parents in Indianapolis.

"Never again," she said, propping her feet up on the dash.

"It wasn't so bad."

Now the South came in thick and choppy through the open windows. He loved to drive. She didn't think he should (climate!), but what an experience, the roads of this country. It was stomach-turning, really, how roomy a nation could be. The interstate was god. Anand believed. He'd grown up in the kind of metropolis where traffic sorts itself into sedimentary layers, socialist-era cars fanning out to rickshaws, bicycles, cows, goats, chickens, foot traffic, loiterers, schoolkids, scooters that darted every which way, honking at the schoolmarm signs: *No horns!* Once, during a period of communal unrest, his cab driver had tapped a man's thigh with the car. He'd nearly run him over. Such accidents were more common than Diana might have guessed. The real mistake had been getting out of the vehicle to check on the pedestrian in the gathering crowd, when tensions were so high . . .

CCR whined from the dash.

There was hardly any foot traffic in this country, certainly not on Jefferson Davis Highway.

"Slow down," Diana cried, as he wedged the rental between two semis. "Slow down, slow down, slow down!"

No matter where they drove, what borders they crossed, Anand preferred to traverse new terrain with guidebooks, apps, recommendations solicited from email chains and message boards. Museum tours were researched in advance and audio guides reserved. This was a major difference between them. It was to Diana's great relief, then, arriving at Gettysburg earlier that morning, that the museum was fresh out of auditory apparatuses. She'd gone to the car to change her shirt while Anand had made absolutely sure. They'd commenced, regretfully or mercifully, depending on your perspective, with nothing but their phones.

One did not have high hopes for Gettysburg. Nor for Pennsylvania in general. Having grown up in Indiana, Diana felt she'd earned her condescension. It broadcast her distance. But Gettysburg was on the way and in the end had outperformed. They exited the visitor center and into the scorch of national lore. It was hard to see, in such weather, the advantage of wool uniforms.

"Actually—"

"I'm joking, it was a joke," she said.

The battlefield lay across a narrow road. They paused to allow a sky-blue pickup truck to pass. The driver also slowed, stopped, looked them over. After a halting pause—should they, shouldn't they, would he squash them to a pulp?—he waved them across.

The sun was high, the air heaving and humid. The heat formed a blister over the grass. Outside a modest whitewashed house, the kind of structure raised in a day by horse and rope, they read a little plaque. Here was Union HQ, it said. Ahead, the lawn descended the gentle slope that had given General Meade such a historically significant edge. They stood there an extra beat, rereading the same sentences multiple times. Anand suppressed a smile.

"What's so funny?"

"Same to you."

She laughed. "Nothing's funny."

It came to light that they'd both been wondering what the driver of the pickup had thought about a couple like them.

Even someone with zero knowledge of military strategy (and this was Diana to a fault) could recognize, standing atop the knoll, how terribly advantageous it was to defend an attack from above. You could see everything. (There, in the distance, were the woods where the Confederates had chilled themselves, sleeping in the dew in nonwicking cotton.) In the scant shade of a copse, a guide was addressing a pair of women at opposite extremes of the weight distribution: a thin, nervous-looking specimen tried so hard to disappear beneath her sun hat that you couldn't help but stare, while her capacious friend radiated a generous attention. (If Diana had had a musket, she thought, neither would stand a chance.) Anand consulted the map. The thing to do was walk across the field, clamber over the fence, and peek into the woods where the Confederates had begun their charge. It really was quite a ways to march. Off they went. They clambered. They arrived. They peered into the trees.

"That's that."

On their return, by the copse, another memorial plaque made an appearance; on it, someone had laid a bouquet in honor of fallen Confederates. The roses were a deep, expensive red. Anand shook his head.

In the car, hours later and hundreds of miles south, a deep sunburn bloomed across Diana's shoulders.

"I wore long sleeves!"

"Should've tried wool!"

Anand thought it very strange that Diana had never met her uncle, especially as she had no other uncles or aunts or cousins to meet. "That's wild," he'd said, when he found out. Diana shrugged. She hadn't met a lot of her family.

"Salt and vinegar, or sour cream and onion?"

She handed Anand more napkins for his lap and popped open the tube of chips. (Sour cream and onion.) He was probing the matter again, she felt, like a kid left alone on the beach with a stick. Was it an argument, an affair, an inheritance dispute? She snorted, spewing crumbs.

"What inheritance!"

It was none of these things.

She turned to the trees and gas stations of the anonymous landscape outside. "I did visit once. Right after college. I drove all the way down. He didn't show. So, I guess don't get your hopes up."

Together, Jefferson Davis and Anand drew the rest of the story out of her. The truth was, there had a been a cousin once, seven years her senior, whom she'd also never met. This too was wild. Was it? She was used to silences. It was much more like her family to let things lie. The cousin had died at fourteen of a rare strain of blood cancer. It was too hard on everyone, in the following years, to present another little girl who reminded them so much of her.

"Honestly, maybe we shouldn't. I can look up the motel I stayed in last time. It had a pool."

Diana reached for her phone. Anand covered the screen.

"It's a good thing to do," he said. "I'm proud of you."

She cradled the chips. "Maybe just keep your eyes on the road."

The remaining facts she knew about the uncle were few. For example, he was the only other person in her family to have earned a college degree. In the arts, specifically, courtesy of the GI Bill and the Korean War. Active duty had left him a little eccentric. It was his degree, however, that her parents most commented on. Her own mother was a typist, skilled enough in shorthand to have chanced Chicago, where she'd met Diana's father, a bridge player at the time. He played professionally for years before earning his accounting license. Neither had seen the point of university back then, but pity the person who thought it was because they hadn't been clever enough. When Diana had come home junior year chattering about her history thesis ("Messianic Expectations in Socialist Yugoslavia, 1929–1992"), her father had remarked, not a little saltily, "Sounds like a load of overintellectualized bullshit to me." It had stung at the time. But she'd been all of twenty, and her father wasn't quite wrong. Though, following the logic through, that still didn't make him right.

Her father had performed many jobs over the years. Taxi driver. Lab assistant. Bookkeeper. Carpenter. He was rather proud of Diana, she knew, whether or not he had the words, and frankly she was proud of him, too. The problem was expressing it. The problem was that she felt ashamed of her parents at times, or perhaps the better word was confused. She didn't know how to place them. It was like showing up for dinner with an unruly bouquet to find the host keeps only a delicate little vase. The first time her parents had met Anand, over tourist spaghetti in Manhattan ("Miserable fucking city," was her father's—again—not totally incorrect pronouncement), they'd complimented his English, by which they meant that they were surprised that he spoke it much better than they did. "Thanks," Anand said. "It is definitely my first language." He added that a lot of the students back home spoke better English than their teachers, who came from more modest backgrounds. Her parents nodded, uncomprehending. Diana considered drowning herself in her personal vat of spaghetti.

The exit appeared. She held out a chip to Anand. He ate it out of her hand. "Narm narm num," he articulated.

A final thing Diana knew about her uncle was that her own college tuition had been drawn from the fund her cousin had never had the chance to use. After she died, it had sat there, accruing interest, for eleven intervening years.

"It's nothing to feel guilty about," Anand said.

It really was a beautiful country, as long as you had no memory. Wrung of its history, the land greets its visitors with the complete indifference of a stolen thing.

The uncle lived on a cul-de-sac in a neighborhood comprised of what had once been called starter homes but which now bore the signs of urban decay. The sky was still and gray when they arrived, draped ominously low over the roofs. The house sat on a respectable stretch at the far edge of the development, abutting a strip of trees. The driveways were designed for one car each, though most held two, none of them new.

She would have been able to guess which was her uncle's even without the address. Part of her still hoped she was mistaken.

Improvised sculptures were staked all over the weedy lawn. The majority were abstract. One was definitely a shotgun. The hedges at the door were not so much hedges but brush, and the house was in visible disrepair. The eaves sank; the roof buckled; the shingles were ripe with moss. After decades sculpting models for a local automobile plant, now her uncle lived alone and made the art he liked, apparently in vast quantities. His wife, much younger, had left after their daughter died.

At the door, Diana knocked. Anand followed with the bags.

"No one home?"

"Looks like no."

"I'm sure he'll come."

They sat on the front step to wait.

Anand was correct. It wasn't long before her uncle made his memorable entrance. He sped in on a dirt bike in a flurry of dust and growling noise. The brakes throttled backwards; his was the torso of a much younger man. Diana had only ever seen a picture, and that he'd seemed handsome then was confirmed again as he removed the helmet with its long, pointed chin. His white hair was full and cropped, his features set deep in a face almost gaunt. Diana was grateful Anand remained so reliably delicate when it came to first impressions.

"Wow," he said. "Nice bike."

Thirty minutes later, her uncle was leading Anand in circles around the house, teaching him to ride. It had never occurred to Diana that riding a motorcycle—"Sorry, sorry, *not* a motor-cycle . . . !"—required so much balance. There were no three-wheeled dirt bikes, of course, and one had to start somewhere. It certainly made a racket. She kept waiting for one of the neighbors to come out and complain, but either they were used to it or they had fled long ago. Anand, straddling the roaring engine, tapped along the green on tiptoe, weaving through the crowded sculpture garden whose rusted copper shapes erupted in teal and pink and orange. Her uncle, at his elbow, guided him patiently. So patiently, in fact, that it was almost as if he didn't want to go inside. It was dark by the time Anand was able to circle the cul-de-sac on his own. Still parked on the front steps, Diana clapped when he pulled into the drive. Her uncle lumbered over. A silence swelled with the ridiculous things neither could bring themselves to say: *Nice to meet you . . . So here we are . . . Uh, thanks for paying my tuition . . .* Diana drummed her hands on her thighs.

Her uncle spat thickly into the bushes. "You sure you don't want to try?"

The house was crammed with family pictures and more art, two bedrooms, and a bath wedged between. Diana set out her toothbrush and face wash and expensive creams at the sink. She reapplied some much-needed deodorant. Anand was in their room, humming eighties hits from their road trip playlist and setting out a change of clothes. Back home, in high school, he'd played briefly in a cover band; he broke fully into song.

"Maybe if you joined a *different* band—"

"If you want an autograph, just ask."

"The very occasional silence can also be harmonious."

The purple bed was piled with pillows, as if a seasonal sale were going on: last call for throw cushions in aisle four. A border of ivy crawled along the baseboards. It was undoubtedly a little girl's room. The violet plush of the carpet crunched, stiff with lack of use.

Diana shouldered her purse and surveyed the luggage. "Is my bag still in the car?"

"I thought you brought yours in yourself."

The asphalt released the day's heat into the night. Diana hopped from one bare foot to the other in the driveway, looking into the rental trunk. No luck.

In the purple bedroom, they backtracked, recreating the afternoon. It had been so hot and clear in Gettysburg: while Anand was inquiring as to the audio guide options, she'd returned to the car for long sleeves to avoid the very sunburn she'd nevertheless incurred. She mimed opening the trunk of the rental car:

"—I took out my bag—"

"—and put it where?—"

"—and then I took off the shirt I was wearing—"

"—right in the middle of the parking lot?—"

"—and then—"

"—and then you put on *this* shirt?—"

"—obviously, and then—"

"—you put the bag back?"

Diana lowered herself to the foot of the bed, her head into her hands. "Honestly, how did you not run over it?"

"Sorry for being such a careful driver!"

She lifted her collar to her nose. "I'm already starting to smell."

It was too late to call the museum. With a sinking feeling, she recalled the public transit warnings in New York: all that lost baggage, needlessly destroyed. She stripped and curled up next to Anand in the bed dressed for a child.

"I hate sleeping naked in other people's homes."

Laughing, he reached for her.

"No, seriously, it's weird."

That she'd never known all that much about her family came into focus in the wide-angle lens of adulthood. She didn't *know* her family better. But she understood them in a different light. In certain settings or times of day (a party, her office hours, departmental committees), her forebearers were recognized as workers, and worthy of praise; everything real in this country had been produced by hand, preferably an American's. And yet, as the background sets changed, these very same cafeteria managers, FedEx couriers, self-trained accountants and small-time entrepreneurs now played the knave, not so much the salt of the earth as the runoff that had poisoned it: the kind of people who'd voted, in an act of willful self-annihilation, for the incorrect president.

Diana was *fairly* confident her uncle hadn't. She weighed the evidence lying in bed. He wasn't an especially enthusiastic citizen. He tended to forget to pay his taxes (as she knew from the occasions her father had been called in to help), which of course caused trouble with the law, which in turn introduced in him certain biases against the government. So there was that issue, were he to vote. Though she wagered lack of civic interest had probably won out. Lying awake, still inappropriately naked and decidedly unaroused, she listened to the easy sounds of the storm. Envied Anand his sleep. He wrapped a leaden arm around her. It weighed heavily on her breasts. Gently, she removed it. The eaves shuddered. She stared at the ceiling fan. Ideally she'd have had the chance to prepare her uncle the way she had her parents, to coach him on those things that were and weren't appropriate to say to someone who had grown up elsewhere and only recently become American. The whole world is a reason to worry at 4 a.m. She pushed herself up from the bed and slipped on her filthy shirt, her wrinkled linen uniform.

Half an hour later, she was at the sink in the kitchen, nursing a cup of leftover coffee she'd found languishing in the globe of the Mr. Coffee pot. The mesh of Anand's basketball shorts breathed around her knees. His sweet voice still spun in her head—unfortunately what it sang was CCR. She watched the storm. She was about to search the cupboards for snacks or go out to the car for the rest of the chips when the side door snapped open. Her uncle entered from the garage.

There are two kinds of guests, those who naturally make themselves at home, and those perpetually ashamed creatures horrified to be caught doing anything in any room. Diana was of the latter variety, which is to say her uncle's arrival startled her completely. He was speaking softly to a Pyrex tray of raw chicken thighs. The oven clock cast the pallid skins in a lunar glow.

Diana splashed some water at the coffee she'd spilled onto her shirt.

"Hello?"

"The fox . . . the fox . . ." he said.

Diana's father often sleepwalked. It must be hereditary. This was a tender thought. She knew just what to do. She took the tray and set it on the counter, so that her uncle's hands now loosely gripped the air. She affirmed everything he said. "The fox, the fox of course, let's get you back to bed." She directed him back into the hall, past all the pictures of his daughter, here posing with a papier-mâché volcano; here in the woods with her little crossbow; here on Christmas in a green velvet dress draped with a wide ribbon sash.

They were at the entrance to his bedroom when he came to. She watched him take in the time, her shorts, her soaked-through shirt.

"That's quite the outfit."

"I left my bag in Gettysburg."

Her uncle puzzled a moment longer. She had the feeling of backing into someone else's nightmare. Then, without warning, he threw back his head and laughed. The response was so alarming she doubted his lucidity. He wiped his eyes.

"Oh yeah, *I Left My Bag in Gettysburg*, I saw that on Broadway opening night."

How was it that *she* was always pegged the hysterical one? Diana returned to bed in a huff. When she woke, the sky was clear, and Anand was just stepping out of the shower, fresh back from a run.

"Cool shorts," he said.

Looking down, she saw she'd fallen asleep atop the duvet in the mesh, while he had gone running in his nice cotton ones.

What do you do with an uncle you've never met? Luckily the storm had left them with several chores. Outside, driftwood was strewn over the sculpture garden. They helped to gather it, collecting the branches into neat piles. Then her uncle looked at the sky and said, "Screw it," because the next storm, signposted in the gathering clouds, would only nuke them again. They cooked the chicken legs to feed the fox who often lingered at the stream, and who was also fed handfuls of peanuts and blueberries. "Foxes eat this?" Of course they did. For lunch the humans too ate chicken legs, hot and unseasoned and dripping with fat, consumed while standing up around the same glass tray. They balanced bones in fingertips. "Fucking delicious!" her uncle said. It was hard not to want to tell an octogenarian to take it easy, hard not to tell him to try, at least, to be a little cautious. He'd survived the Korean War, prostate cancer, a dislocated spine. He'd fallen from the platform where he'd been sighting deer and temporarily paralyzed both legs. Could Anand or Diana have army-crawled back to the car to keep warm until the ambulance arrived? Could they have performed a deadweight pull-up from the ground to reach the driver's seat? The uncle thought not. Anand leaned on his rake. "Agree to disagree."

He and Diana looked around the yard at the sawhorse, woodshed, dirt bike, tools, the sculptures advancing between the woodpiles like opposing pieces on a chessboard. It was true they were unused to this line of work, to this part of the world. It was enough to scramble your brain. Diana paused to sniff again at the collar of her rancid shirt. With a look either conciliatory or cunning—it was hard to tell with him—her uncle turned to Anand.

"You know what you could help me with," he said. And without further ado, he disappeared around the side of the house.

They found him in the garage at the workbench beside the extra oven he'd installed for cooking in bulk (for the fox?), which excluded the possibility of being able to park a car. Car or no car, he'd always lusted after one of those automatic doors. Now over eighty, he conceded, eventually his back would go, and this time not so temporarily. He held out the hardware to Anand. The box read *EZ Glide!*.

"You people are all so handy with IT—"

Diana snatched at the device as if it were a grenade he was about to detonate.

"I'll do it, I'll do it," she said.

Halfway up the ladder, electric screwdriver in hand, instruction booklet crumpled on the floor, Diana began to question her gallantry. She listened to her uncle's welding tips filter through the kitchen door. One detected the cracking open of beers. Now he was inviting Anand to see the basement studio—"Where the magic happens!"—an incantation soon followed by the heavy creak of two grown men descending wooden steps. A creeping jealousy, not entirely unfamiliar, seeped into her chest. The truth was, her family often seemed more comfortable when Anand was around. He had this effect on people. He was easily loved. Whole dinner parties courted his attention. It was obviously one of many reasons she'd fallen in love with him herself; why she was still surprised he'd fallen for her. He appeared more at ease than she was in either of their respective worlds, plus the third they shared. She envied how he drew her parents out. They glowed, flattered; the world had come to them. The initial friction overcome, these days they addressed themselves to him, not their daughter, when the four of them convened. "I'm sure that's not true," Anand had said, a statement quickly retracted at the look of protest on her face. "Okay, okay, but I'm sure it's not intentional." There was maybe even a mutual anthropological interest there. She couldn't help now but resent that it was Anand down in the studio with her uncle, to whom he had encouraged her to introduce herself against her every intuition. She notched the electric screwdriver against the wooden frame of the garage and pressed with all her might. At the very least, she would figure out this fucking door. That was for sure. The drill bit sank into the wood. The lintel bracket was secured. Then the drill caught, sputtered, and crashed, ejecting the battery into the drainage grate. Diana, for her part, was left swinging from the lip of the frame, one foot on the ladder, the other flailing free. She caught her breath, her balance, briefly contemplated her uncle's experience with paralysis. It occurred to her that she could not perform a pull-up of any kind.

Then again, she hadn't fallen.

Steadying herself, she shifted the ladder to connect the power unit. The contraption blinked. Slowly, the door folded into itself, disgorging the heat of the stilted afternoon. In the dark, the overhead light flickered on.

.

She was high with success! In the way only very unhandy people are at the first sign of savoir faire. It was a rush. She was feeling, all in all, not exactly herself. Her arms ached with the effort of holding the screwdriver aloft, her heart flooded with adrenaline from her close call. She could feel the sweat and salt on the surface of her skin. And something else, beneath it. She listened to the silence of the house. Her uncle and Anand were still in the cellar. It hardly bothered her anymore.

At the sink, she wrung out her shirt, then splashed her face and underarms and glanced into the mirror. The body there was soft and fragile, completely unsuited to the capable person she suddenly felt herself to be. Oh well. Mirrors lie. Her clothes dripping from the shower rod, she planted herself before the closet doors. The handles were brass blooms, and she harvested them in her palms. Rows and rows of garments appeared, in more or less her size but in better taste. Their curator had been very careful, she realized. Diana passed an admiring hand along the hems. She'd no idea her cousin, older by seven years, or else younger by twenty-three, had cultivated such a precocious style. Perhaps she could have taught Diana a thing or two. This imaginary thread cast itself into the past and immediately fell slack. She lifted the sleeve of a gingham shirtdress and let it fall. There were shoulder pads in the jackets and silk linings in the skirts. She was reminded of a novel she'd once read set in colonial Hong Kong, in which a notorious doyenne attempts to turn her school-age niece into a concubine. It's for her own good; the niece's prospects are grim. The girl makes her way uphill in the swampy summer, thrashing through the vegetation to the aunt's opaline palace at the crest. In her new bedroom she opens the wardrobe to a rackful of party dresses. There are outfits for every occasion, tailored right down to her slender, still adolescent waist. Lavender sachets tucked inside each collar keep the garments fresh. Where would she ever wear them? The girl knew immediately, and in spite of her better instincts, that she'd been bought. It was too late; she was in too deep.

In the approaching mid-Atlantic storm, the room was almost tropical; there was no more use in Diana's resisting the wardrobe. Still, something in her hesitated. She wished to ask permission. Then again, there were at least thirty dresses here. Odds were her uncle wouldn't notice. The residue from her shower still clung to her collarbone, and the gingham checks blossomed as she slipped the shirtdress on. She cinched the waist. It was a perfect fit.

The cellar access was hazardously steep and led directly from the kitchen. From the oven, in fact. Opening the appliance door to check the clearance, Diana was launched onto the landing. She stood there. The men's voices rose up to meet her. Anand was asking polite questions (How had he gotten started? What was this machine? Perhaps a demonstration?). Then, after a while, he no longer was. It was just her uncle speaking.

One did not harbor high hopes for her uncle's studio (one had seen the lawn), but that's not what this descent was about now, was it? She lowered herself onto the top step. He wasn't talking about art anymore. Or maybe he was. What did she know? Her father was right. What a real bullshitter she was.

She turned an ear to the cellar depths. It was the war that had risen to the surface of the conversation there, like oil on the highway after rain. Her uncle had been stationed in the trenches along the 38th Parallel. (Cartographers are the true warmongers.) His tone was distant, as if the memory were speaking of its own, disembodied accord. It wasn't easy to describe, he said, what it was like to survive only just barely in touch with your limbs. Imagine

Christmas Eve. The perspective is age eighteen. Everything sinks. Boots. The men inside of them. They disappear into the snow. The Chinese are blasting carols across no man's land. This was the void: hearing "Jingle Bell Rock" in a trench in the dead of night in a proxy war at the end of the world. Maybe it wasn't "Jingle Bell Rock." But it should have been. Could any carol make a better weapon? The point was he needed no reminder of the reasons to fear his country. He'd seen its pulsing heart, packed in bloody snow. A note of hysteria laced his story now. He asked Anand, "You sing?" He'd had his own way with music once, he said. As did every kid back then. You played the campsites until the draft letter came, then left the instrument and your old man's disappointments behind. A shivery tremor sang out. Diana descended.

Her uncle stood beneath the basement's single exposed bulb, holding a sonorous sheet of copper. It rang triumphant, like a gong. Anand sat on the workbench, looking as if he too had just survived a tour. He watched Diana arrive. Following his gaze, her uncle turned. Who was this apparition at the bottom of the stairs? For the first time, he struck Diana as old. She drew up a stool. Without protesting, he sat. His chin fell to his chest. She knelt to check his pulse and pupils. They were in accord. In her head, a horrid clanging chorus. She demonstrated deep breaths. "Come on, you too," she said. He patted her hands with his. It was the gesture of an elderly man. His eyes were clouded yet clear, like an early sky; soon the heat would burn away the fog. The crisis was not of medical origin, she decided, but something more obscure. "I'm sorry," she said. "I left—" Yes, yes, the musical. He breathed in. It took ages. She hooked an arm under his. "Up, up then, let's go upstairs." Again, he didn't protest. His weight against her was totally insignificant, as if the fate of every body were a slow evaporation; eventually, we disappear, a bit more humidity released into the air.

Anand, still listening from the workbench, heard Diana say, "You've got yourself an automatic garage door now."

They got her uncle to bed. It was midafternoon, and the daylight felt foreign after the basement. They retreated into their own ersatz room, where Anand drew the curtains.

"That was intense."

He collapsed onto the pillows, and Diana followed suit. They lay side by side in the restrained sun. Diana's legs were folded, uncouthly froglike, under the hem of her dress.

"Did you know any of that?"

She didn't respond. He kissed her. Pressing himself into her, he felt the new sharpness of her bones and wondered when it was she'd lost so much weight. How rudely people change. Though she pulled him close, touching him the way he liked, something stayed stiff and unyielding inside the gingham. He had a hand in the skirt, exploring essences, before he too gave up. The entire affair felt wrong for reasons that were vague on the whole but intuitive in the particulars. "These fucking pillows." He tossed one to the floor and put his warm hands to his ribs. "I feel a little sick." Diana smoothed his face. Stroked his sweaty temples.

"Come on," she said. "You haven't seen the garage yet."

They stood barefoot on the cool cement, watching the door unfold itself again and again, a gigantic lolling tongue. "You did good." "I know!" She punched the remote and the garage growled to a tight-lipped state. They watched it open and close, open and close. The mechanics left them hungry. They went out to feed the fox, then themselves. From the kitchen window, they watched the vixen nudge the bowl they'd left by the overflowing stream, all the while shoveling handfuls of blueberries and peanuts into their own mouths. "I could live like this," she said. "I'm starving," said Anand. They were two children who've stumbled on an abandoned house in the woods, eager to see what the owners have left behind. A box of pasta, a can of tomatoes. Onions and garlic sprouted behind the pantry door.

The radio switched on, announcing her uncle's return. He emerged from the bedroom with boom- and pillbox tucked under his arm. In the kitchen, he slipped a CD into the plate, then counted out a permutation of pale capsules and washed them down. There were good days and bad days, he explained, and many in between. The wind picked up. The storm unfurled luxuriously, like a dark sheet of crushed silk. The table crowded with heaping bowls of pasta and rows of votive candles. Anand sat across from Diana. She flickered in the candlelight, still in her gingham dress. The music was far too loud for conversation, you could hardly hear the wind. When the power went out, the world plunged into a 24-karat darkness. The battery-powered Beach Boys clanged on. Something of that bandstand genius, Anand thought, echoed in every American song. Diana's uncle asked for bread. The gingham strained horribly against her breasts as she passed it to him—she was a woman, this was a child's garment. The exchange precipitated a housewife's loving look. Anand dropped his eyes.

The car keys were in his pocket, and he registered their weight as the chorus spun around once more. Here was the music, the storm, the inertia, the heat, the awful commotion of a single discography set eternally on repeat. Kilometers of highway stretched ahead. But it was far too late; he was in too deep.

GHOST PAINS

That evening, convening downtown with a set she'd known since school, Tina was struck by a powerful burst of pride. A group of five or six of them was walking east from the bar where she'd topped off two beers with a dirty martini, just to show she could. With the blessing of the streetlights, a certain Dave was trying to convince the new girl to give him her number, and Tina felt her own courage swell. (They'd taken linear algebra together, shared eigenvalues; she too could be transformed.) "I'm starving," someone said. "I'm not," said Tina, "but I know a spot." The piercing shop she had in mind was just down the street, tucked beneath a Dollar Slice, and they made two stops for the trouble of one. That was the fundamental philosophy—more bang for your buck—of the dollar pizza slice. Oh, the chorus of everyone she knew: You're not the type! She resolved to show them otherwise, at one or maybe three in the morning, as she sank back into the reclining chair, lifted her shirt, and allowed the piercing artist to notch the gun around the pink tip of a breast. ("Yes, just one.") She resolved to show herself: she was in fact exceedingly able when it came to excruciating situations. That's what type she was. After all, college. After all, life. All these years, she'd been rather in love with Dave herself. The pain was sour and slower than expected. Through the halo of it, she spotted her friends.

"Ouch," Dave said in solidarity, slipping an arm around the new girl as the little barbell went in.

It is human nature to overestimate ourselves. In the bar down the block, the one she'd always thought of as Polish but was in fact run by Ukrainians, the friends ordered pitchers. She went to the restroom to look into the mirror. The usual disappointment. In her breast, she was experiencing what can only be described as an existential throb. She took a break on the urine-caked tiles. The friends were just on the other side of the wall, but at that moment they seemed very far away, mere approximations of people she'd known. Leaning her head against the sink pipe, she wondered, as she did once a melodramatic month or so, What if I died right here, right now? But as previously mentioned, she knew her way around a bit of pain. That was her schtick. The thing to do was breathe until the room steadied itself and the tremor faded on the Richter scale, going, going, gone, stabilizing into a single plane across which her chic friends were calling, *Tina, are you okay?!*

It was a good party trick, this nipple bar of hers. Those who found out about it never saw her quite the same. *Oh . . . really?* It drew people (men) in. Who were any of us to know what type others were or weren't?

She moved through her twenties, gathering evidence. She met a financier not without a sadomasochistic streak himself: in the millisecond during which pork bellies dipped, he swooped in and bought up bellies, reselling them at a premium of one hundredth of a cent, having fleetingly driven up demand. It was a thrilling, precise, and algorithmic matter of legally dubious finesse. "Oh," Tina said. "I wouldn't know, I work in tech." Here was a hotel bar of a kind she was only very recently able to afford after paying off her student loans, and where, looking over her cocktail at the history professor she'd met online, it became clear that whatever type *he* was, it wasn't hers; he'd written an undergraduate thesis on Weimar whores. "Is that an academic subject?" He laughed. "Very good! That's good. Of course, fascism as sexual fetish." It's hard to tell when German historians are joking. Maybe it's just the accent.

Out of a perverse desire to befriend the women her love interests had chosen over her, she courted Dave's new girl, no longer new, which led to a threesome, and then to tears, culminating in Tina's regrettable exile. Finally, on date four or five, a promising composer of slot machine jingles—the goal was movie scores—posed the fatal question: "You mean to tell me you are mathematically inclined, not baptized, of Polish extraction, and you're *not* a member of the Tribe?" Only on her in-laws' side, where all her cousins had been mitzvahed. Alas, conversion failed to leap bloodlines. Sometimes these exes called up too late to ask, "What are you doing right now?" "I'm soaking my nipple in salt water." "What?" She repeated, *"I'm soaking my nipple piercing!"*

Tina never was very good at lying.

I don't need to tell you how these relationships came to an end. The dates always started out perfectly nice. Tina was more or less in thrall. In another life, by now she has kids and a house; the composer arranges his movie scores. As things stood, however, there was always too much history between them, sexual and other-wise. It got in the way of her every attempt at love. Particularly culpable were the mixed signals generated by the nipple piercing. Like a magnetic field, it threw her suitors off. She'd given Rob, the kinky historian, a key to her apartment so that he could visit more often, then at night, when she was already asleep. He liked to open the door gently, gently, and surprise her in her dreams. The scene seemed asymptotically related to assault, but such is the nature of the asymptote: meaningful equivalence takes a long time. She thought of this, six months in, when, sensing her sudden hesitation, he stopped and sat up, bashing his head on the sloping and frankly hazardous ceiling.

"Well, don't just *lie there!*" he yelled.

She directed him across the room to the kitchen for an ice pack. For a long time afterward, she would be able to recall the image of him there, naked in front of the open freezer door, a purple ice penguin pressed against his head.

She regretted falling out with those old friends. How many of them had been priced out, moved upstate, moved home. She got up and washed her hair, crawled back into bed with her phone. All those years ago, she'd been so sure she would have her life figured out by now. It had seemed an inevitable process, answering the dogged question, *Really, what kind of person . . . ?* Instead it had turned out to be one unending mystery. Very much dependent on context.

The nipple bar never really healed, by the way. That's what you get for choosing the only place open at 3 a.m. On the subway, she struck a protective stance. The pain was faint, but when it arrived, it yanked her back into the past, and always at unexpected moments. She took these as cosmic signs. Time to leave the city was what they said. And so, five years later, she did.

Tina was good at her job. The transfer was hers for the taking when the opportunity arrived. So it was that, five years later again, she stepped out of Warsaw International and onto the train plat-form. She had in her pocket one first-class ticket. She was bound for Krakow, direct.

No one else seemed to be headed to Krakow that day. The train was empty. She of course was traveling on business. The office wanted to know if Poland was the next Lithuania or Ukraine,

that is, a cradle for start-ups incubating world-class talent on dis-
counted pay. She knew more about the country than most, true, but
she suspected she'd seemed the appropriate choice due to the con-
sonants crammed into her name. ("Yes, both sides—Chicago and
Detroit.") Her other purpose for traveling was nostalgia of a type
that didn't really belong to her. Gliding beneath the gray silk of the
sky, through snowy fields (was this cabbage country, or wheat?), she
tried to recall her grandfather's descriptions. One of the last things
he'd said to her before he died was that being American meant she
didn't have to dwell so much in the past. That was the advantage.
Yes, she had wanted to add, but couldn't they have also dwelt a
little more? The doors of the train car opened with an automated
pfft, and a woman came down the aisle, very busy on her phone.
Tina returned to the window. The contours of the war, as gleaned
from her relatives, had only ever been revealed in the negative, a
pattern scissored from the dossier of all the other, more practical
things they'd said. (That the ones she'd met had said, that is.) She
pulled out her laptop. Traveling 40 percent of the time left one in
a state of contemplative dislocation conducive to reflections like
these. It filled in the silence.

The first thing she did after checking in to her hotel was to buy a
pack of cigarettes and wander over the cobblestones to the nearest bar, where she ordered two fried discs of mountain cheese. A
pilsner arrived. The beer was blonde, the wood was blonde, and
so was the waitress who brought her food. A soccer match was
on, and she watched the jerseys flash white and ruby across the
screen. Eating alone is a consultant's art, and key criteria include
a view of the television and proximity to a table whose conversation carries in a language you can understand. That night, Tina

found herself adjacent to an animated set speaking in English to accommodate the single American, a student studying abroad. She ate very slowly. The wrong team scored. The party next to her was becoming increasingly inflamed over the Iraq War. The American cursed his own government. The Poles, his allies, cursed theirs. On screen, white rallied and the game was tied. Fans at the bar raised their glasses and cheered. It was into this commotion that the door swung wide open, trailing a swirl of snow.

The man who entered was smartly dressed and vaguely familiar. His clothes cut so close that at first she mistook him for Swiss or French. His gait, however, betrayed the far-flung tourist's hesitance. The shoulders slumped. She realized then she'd seen those shoulders before. For an entire semester of linear algebra. Also, far more intimately, wedged between the new girl's thighs. Before she knew it, before all available options had been properly weighed, as might befit a consultant of her experience, Tina had ducked beneath the table as soundlessly as a swimmer pulled under a wave.

Tina hadn't seen Dave in a long while. Not since the attempt to torpedo his relationship had—she could admit it now—succeeded only in sinking herself. Perhaps she was mistaken? From under the table, she watched the waitress's white pumps click across the floorboards as her half-finished plate was whisked away. The cheese—! That was a shame. Fans cheered as someone scored—she'd have to watch the replay. It was part of her job to keep up with sports. She breathed in the sticky pilsner scent. Despite her extensive HR training, Tina had never fully bought into trigger warnings, or at the very least had supposed them tangential to her own experience; everyone had close calls. And yet here she was, under a table in a foreign country, hands wrapped around her knees, a cheap ring stamping itself unattractively onto her forehead. A pair of practical boots appeared, replacing the waitress's pumps.

"Tina?"

"Oh, hello."

Dave looked at her for a long moment. "I thought that was you!" he said.

There are certain people for whose arrival one would like to be prepared: Hitler; your mother-in-law; yourself when you're high and suddenly confronted by a mirror. The best you can do is be constantly on guard against such unpleasantness, overprepared to be shocked, and therefore not, when the moment finally arrives. The thing to do was act naturally, as if the past had never happened.

"Great to see you," Tina said.

She accepted his hand and his invitation, followed him to the bar.

They sipped in silence. Another game passed. When the match finished, there was nothing to do but stare at the ads. Dave had been supporting the losing team, and because their last meeting had not ended on especially fine terms, Tina had pretended to support them too. Now they both had lost.

"Well, fuck."

"Brutal," she agreed.

He asked her what she was doing here in Krakow and she explained for too long, lingering over all the mind-numbing details. The start-ups. The talent search. The race to hire the best from this part of the world before competing firms caught on. She hadn't imagined winding up in headhunting. It sounded so violent. "I'm not exactly a people person." That he knew. "But compared to most programmers, I guess I seem emotionally intelligent. What about you?"

Dave stared at the foam at the bottom of his mug. "Restitution for my grandfather's apartment. He died last month, so."

At a loss for what to say, Tina ordered another pilsner. A tooth whitening ad bleached the screen. "Cigarette?" He took one. Later, when she reached for her purse, he placed a hand on hers. A few złoty fell to the blonde, blonde wood.

"Please," he said. "Honestly, it's good to see someone."

Her hotel was a few blocks away, a brief turn through the snow. The night was navy and the snowbanks glowed cerulean, duplicitous and strange. They stood for a moment outside the lobby, Dave kicking lightly at the icy crusts.

Tina asked, "Are you still with Sylvia?"

"Nah."

Kick, kick. The silence stretched.

"I'm sorry," he said. "I should have let you be."

"No, really, it's good to see you too." Tina threw up her hands with a little laugh. "Just embarrassing. Embarrassing who I was back then, I mean. Hell, who I am."

He looked at her. She looked at the shifting colors of the snow.

"Poland is full of secrets," he said.

Krakow was quiet that night. It left you alone with your thoughts. Upstairs, Tina ran a washcloth under her arms, between her legs. She dabbed at the piercing, too. Then she got into bed and stared into the dark.

She had met Dave's grandfather, she recalled. It was the old man's ninetieth, and Dave had been worried he wouldn't be able to carry the conversation by himself. They'd been just close enough then for him to ask the favor, just distant enough for her to oblige. In an eleven-story building with an old-fashioned elevator whose door opened on a hinge—she remembered because someone had tried and failed to wedge in an antique dresser, and then everyone had had to take the stairs—they'd eaten Tofutti ice cream by the bowl and watched the news. They'd sung. The grandfather had struck her as an intelligent if distractible man. She remembered a silver pitcher on the mantel, stacks of books at their feet. The windows choked with curtains that seemed not to have been drawn in years.

It occurred to her, not for the first time, that she too must have connections here in Poland, though she'd never taken the initiative to look. Her family hadn't always kept in touch, hadn't always gotten along. Her maternal grandmother had been stabbed to death by her very own husband, who'd tired of her requests for child support, who'd tired of Detroit, and so fled back home to Białystok. Rumor had it he kept a second wife. It seemed unwise to track such relations down. Tina flipped on the bedside lamp and reached for the in-flight magazine she'd saved. The glossy pages filled with idle products. Portable grills. Egg timers. It hadn't really hit her until now, and in so many words, that this criminal was related to her. That she was related to him.

She turned the page: dog tags engraved with your beloved's name. She earmarked a discount for a Finnish spa, because her next stop was Lithuania, and Helsinki was just there.

In the morning, the tech conference her firm was sponsoring commenced. The convention hall sucked a few more milliliters from the reservoir of her soul, as if drawing a sample with a syringe. She had no one but herself to blame; she was the MC, after all. It was her responsibility to keep the crowd from becoming suicidally bored. At breakfast tables draped with white tablecloths, coders barely out of university twisted gratis bottles of water. The room erupted with applause, followed by the mangled screech of the plastic vessels being tortured into balls. The tables were set with fake pots of flowers, and the petals fell in rayon blooms as the attendees worried them, too. From the pulpit, Tina concluded the opening session with a toast to the future and splashed a .info@ email onto the projector screen.

She walked back to her hotel through the cold.

The concierge was waiting for her. There was a message—a certain Dave had called. She suppressed a little thrill. How quaint to receive a message through the concierge! He sent her up to her room with a phone number on a slip. It took a few tries to connect.

"Hello?"

In the background, bar sounds. She glanced at the clock. One in the afternoon.

Dave said, "Are you doing anything right now?"

She wasn't due at the conference until tomorrow, which already struck her as too soon.

The legalities of restitution are themselves a kind of exercise in masochism. There was a lot of paperwork involved. Dave explained over lunch beers in the very same bar. One must prove former citizenship for people who've been stripped of it and whose death certificates are liable to have been lost on purpose, or else to lie buried in rural offices in Uruguay, Argentina, or Mexico, in need of translation from the Spanish to the Polish via the English or the original Hebrew. The paradox always was the favorite weapon of the state. Tina tried to keep the respective and competing interests straight. It seemed Dave had worked up a veritable degree in international inheritance, in which field Poland was notoriously ambivalent; it was the only EU member state without a restitution law. Those up for election were liable to claim that it was Germany who ought to foot the bill, including for domestic claims to properties lost in the former Polish territories of Lithuania and Belarus. (Dave's lawyer had stressed that it behooved their case not to frame reclamation as a strictly Jewish issue.) More recently, it was becoming popular to argue that the Germans owed reparations to Poland herself, seeing as how Stalin had siphoned off the previous round. There was the garden-variety blame due the Communists for nationalizing all property in 1945 (*see: Bierut Decree*, said a hot-pink Post-it stuck to the folder containing Dave's copious notes), further complicating questions of inheritance and also of Russia's own involvement. The estimated value of heirless assets seized now hovered, depending on one's sympathies, between thirty and forty billion dollars, or in the individual case of Dave's grandfather's childhood apartment, around two hundred thousand, once converted from the złoty price. On the far-right fringe, international pressure to disambiguate the claims was presented as an anti-Polish scheme cooked up by the Israelis and proxied by the Americans. Tina considered all this. The proliferating Venn diagram of culpability led her back to the conclusion that perhaps the nationalization of property wasn't such a bad idea after all. Recalling the heated arguments she and Dave used to entertain on exactly this topic, and suddenly unsure about the anti-Semitic implications, she kept this Marxist gloaming to herself. She ordered a mountain cheese and grog.

"Good god. You actually like that stuff?"

It was twenty years since Dave's grandfather had first filed a claim, another hour until the appointment with the bureaucrats, during which he would try to argue that the signature on a Paraguayan passport matched that on a marriage certificate drawn up in Polish. A construction crew arrived. With them, a lot of noise. He brought Tina for coffee and no-lunch at a Lonely Planet centerpiece in the city's former Jewish quarter, now quite hip, the guidebook said, known for its nightlife and ethnic specialties, e.g. the sour cherry goose. Tina would have liked to order either cherries or goose—one can only get so far with cheese, especially when one is drinking—but it felt rude to interrupt. The building in question stood just across the street. It was the principle of the thing.

As his legal brief finally drew to a close, a veiled expression settled over Dave's face. Tina recognized it: it was the telltale, jet-lagged dawning of remembering just where you were and why. He checked his watch. Outside, pausing before the contested address, they considered the mullioned windows and the grimy façade. On the uppermost floor, a light turned on, then off.

It was a short walk to the city center, up the steps, through a marbled hall to the lawyer's office where they were scheduled to argue the finer, Paraguayan details of the case. Next was a series of archives to gather deeds and documents; legally, the claim was an inheritance as opposed to a nationalization matter, and so subject to a particularly stringent verification process. Only after his grandfather died did Dave find the contested address, the potential deed, the halted investigation begun two decades prior to his dementia diagnosis. The requirements had become more stringent since.

They clicked across the lobby to the lift.

"So, you speak some Polish?"

Tina's heart sank. She was sorry to reveal the truth, which was that mostly she knew offensive jokes. *How many Poles does it take to change a lightbulb . . . ?* Otherwise, her vocabulary petered out beyond the mainstay of her name. He called the elevator. They bundled in.

"Anyway, thanks for coming."

She was grateful, later, for his having said that, when she reflected that she hadn't been much help at all.

Three hours with the bureaucrats and seventeen new messages awaited her on her phone. She flicked through the banners while walking back to the hotel. The director of the mathematics department at the Lithuanian university wanted to confirm her visit later in the month. The founder of a cryptocurrency had left a message about possible collaboration. A colleague, overly enthusiastic about his work (overly enthusiastic, Tina felt, about her), had just arrived this morning; he'd texted four times, called twice. What was she doing for dinner tonight? It seemed she was forever doomed to attract the wrong sort of person. Meanwhile, the old ache had returned. In line at the pharmacy, Tina made some futile adjustments to her layers of fleece and cashmere. The courthouse had raised her temperature, and now she was cold with sweat.

She charged the saline solution to the company card.

In her room, she struggled with the shower knobs, hot versus cold, the plungers to redirect the water flow, gave up and settled for a bath. While the tub filled, she mixed warm saline in a complimentary cup, then leaned over the counter to soak. She rose and looked at herself, the one breast red, the other coolly lunar, untouched. Ripping open another packet of saline, she mixed a second dose to gargle, because it was flu season, she still had tonsils, and fate did not seem on her side. She felt in desperate need of a deep, internal cleanse.

It wasn't true that she'd been *no* help at the appointment. The truth was far worse: she'd said hardly a word, which had somehow made her seem complicit. At the archives, as Dave argued with the attendant, she'd interjected only to de-escalate. *Would it be possible to . . . ? Could you direct us toward . . . ? Who might be the appropriate point person for . . . ?* "Cunt!" Dave had sworn as they left. Not a workplace-appropriate turn of phrase. Tina was still debating whether he'd said it loud enough for the official to hear. She'd tried to comfort him. "We'll try again tomorrow," she'd said. Stupid. Now, easing herself into her bath, she wished she hadn't.

The piercing—also stupid—was not faring especially well on this trip. It was hard to say why—perhaps it didn't agree with her recent change of bra. Sometimes it responded to the cold, other times to heat, keeping her all too aware of how the barometer of her body expanded, retracted, galvanized attempts to eject foreign objects. Multiple times over the previous decade, she'd considered removing it. She'd considered how different life might have been had she nabbed a sober appointment between the hours of nine and five. A lot had changed. The friends' faces were now vague; they were no longer friends. It was the piercing that remained. It was the friend. It was simply a part of her now.

By the time she went to bed, the third vodka from the minibar was working through her veins. She planted one foot on the floor and her laptop in her lap. The screen cast a soft glow over the furniture, the same Viennese style favored at the Warsaw Bristol, which she'd just left. (That hotel had served as headquarters of the Nazi occupation, leaving it one of the only original buildings still standing in the capital today.) Really, there is nothing like a hotel room when you are drunk and alone to make you feel depressed. A premonition settled thickly over the bed. She navigated to the search bar. Radziłów, Radziłów. Why was the name familiar at all?

The case officer had mentioned it. As she searched, she became increasingly conscious of the encroaching dark, of the anxiety in her chest, the pain in her breast, the memory of her grandfather's (the nice one's) woolen vest, tucked into a piano bench in a family storage unit in Chicago. Of the incriminating combinations of terms accumulating in her browser history. It wasn't pretty to think what kind of data trails she was blazing querying minority populations AND burned alive. That's what had happened in Radziłów, as well as Białystok. In the summer of 1941, volunteers had set fire to a Radziłów barn, Wehrmacht officers to the Białystok Great Synagogue, with entire congregations forced inside. Thousands died. She fell through obscure trapdoors; alighted on questionable domains, Soviet extensions, personal sites that listed the names of the dead, the names of the perpetrators, or at least those whose identities could be hypothesized. Who were the people responsible for these atrocities? Guesses doubled in the lenses of her reading glasses. She cursed the Wi-Fi, searched the family name. Did the arithmetic.

The whole point of tech, Tina sometimes felt, was to remove the friction meant to keep you from indulging the worst in yourself. Then to offer an escape; it was both the illness and the cure. In the end, she texted the colleague back. She agreed to go to dinner with him, a decision she knew she would regret. There is only so much you can deal with alone.

The restaurant turned out, once again, to be Ukrainian. "I'm sick of Polish food!" he announced with American volume as they took their seats. "You just got here," Tina said. He laughed in such a way that brought his body halfway across the table, his face too close to hers. The dining room was a medieval cellar with golden, overpriced lighting that Tina supposed was meant to be romantic. She looked over her menu at the quarter-zip of her colleague's sweater, open to display his tie. The red knot of it presented an appealing bullseye. There was something in him that reminded her of Rob.

It is human nature to overestimate others, at least when estimating from a distance. We can improve, we think. We can surprise each other in pleasant ways. Now that she was actually up close, Tina began the familiar work of adjusting expectations. She lamented once again that, despite the company's self-professed lack of hierarchy, this man was technically her boss's boss. Over hors d'oeuvres, he salivated over rents per square foot of local office space (vacancies hovered at 14 percent) which, when combined with a regional talent force of an estimated 150,000 and average salaries of 30k, made places like Krakow a fairyland for breeding unicorns. He clapped a palm to the tablecloth with such force that the butter lettuce came alive. Tina drew up a mental map. Two hundred kilometers, in almost any direction, brought her out of the country and safely away from her dinner companion. Meanwhile, the thing to do was keep up her buzz. The iron chandelier above her head, wreathed in real candles, fluttered as a waiter passed with an armful of logs. "Excuse me," she said, too quietly. The colleague snapped his fingers. Then he got up, dropping his napkin to his chair. "Yo!"

Tina, resisting the impulse to duck beneath the table once more, ordered a double vodka. She drained it like a champ. If high-functioning alcoholism was all she had inherited from the grandfathers, well, on the whole she'd come out ahead.

It was socially unfortunate, if administratively convenient, that the company housed the whole team in the same hotel. As the meal drew to a close, Rob 2.0 reached for his phone to call a cab.

Tina hesitated. "I think I'll walk back."

"Christ!" he said, with incorrigible cheer.

"No, no, really, you should take a car—"

But he was already gathering his coat. "Into the night!"

They crossed the square and turned down a side street along the old city wall. The trees were stark. A little church, no larger than a New York kitchen, thrust its snowy steeple into the air. The windows melted, an organ swelled; a choir was practicing inside. The beauty of it struck them dumb. When had people lost the habit of singing together? Tina closed her eyes. She wanted to dissolve into the choral hymns. The longer her own silence stretched, however, the more she sensed this man was going to try to kiss her, and clumsily. With great effort she slurred together a few words.

"Do you even like your job?"

Her boss's boss shoved his hands into his pockets and laughed again.

Back at the hotel, as the elevator shuddered to her floor, Tina braced for her escape. He slipped her the extra key card to his room.

"It's very simple, Tina. It's the only thing that's stuck."

The conference was five days in all. It was a long time to avoid your own subconscious, let alone your boss.

After the morning session, the postprandial hours were hers. She was supposed to use them to network, either at the hotel or in one of the myriad coworking spaces deemed so salutary for unicorns. The next day, however, as she cleared the tables of the mangled plastic bottles, too hungover to look at a screen, she felt not at all obliged. When Dave called, she was lying in bed, already in her hat and coat.

"I was going to say, if you—"

"I'll be right there."

And so each day rolled into a copy of the last. That's life. In the morning, pickles, sausages, coffee, more coffee, the plastic screech of the talent as Tina facilitated a *transfer of learning*, transacted a *cultural exchange*, while also reminding everyone that they belonged to the same, borderless community of global leaders in tech. Then came the jotting down of emails belonging to professors and founders and entrepreneurs. Of course they should get a coffee. Of course dinner, everyone has to eat! Wasn't it funny, here again at lunch, to be the only woman, especially when Tina herself was responsible for closing the gender gap? Her boss's boss hooted. "That's how she likes it! Good odds! Ha, ha." Yes, what a novel theory—blame HR. She mixed up the products and personages to which the various emails were assigned. Then to negotiations with the stonewalling bureaucrats, who struck Tina as the real goldmine of talent, the people truly succeeding at their jobs. In these alienating and archival halls, she and Dave worked up a quite literal and anxious sweat. They were received, thwarted, ejected—first politely, then more decisively—back out onto the streets at closing time, where they took half-heartedly to sightseeing. They visited the central square and the museum beneath it, toured the Old Synagogue, Old Town, an overrated buffet, the bookstore with the melting cakes. They cooled off with beers in the blondest of bars. Then home, to solitude and the messages silenced on her phone, the messages waiting with the concierge—

"What?"

"You are 413?"

This time, Tina hesitated. The thrills were getting old:

Tina! STOP Super pres this am STOP Sry for bad joke STOP Made reservation for two at seven STOP Ask

Stanislaw here for address PS it's ITALIAN STOP
STOP STOP

The note was handwritten in what she could only assume was
her boss's boss's hand. She was immediately tempted to take it
to Dave's graphologist. Any sociology in those pastose Ss? The
concierge, however, was eyeing her expectantly from the brassy
depths of the cloakroom, awaiting her reply. She agreed the note
was weird, but there was no simple way of explaining to him that
she did not endorse the message. "Thanks," she said, and retreated
up to her room, where she was received by the laptop and saline and
the impossible taps, with which—now that she was soaking in the
bath—she diverted the flow of her thoughts away from tomorrow
and the day after that, when the interminable cycle would start
again.

STOP

She flipped open the in-flight catalog and contemplated the center
spread of the Finnish spa. Soon enough, she encouraged herself:
Lithuania.

And suddenly there was just one day left.

The idea had occurred to Tina, and perhaps also to Dave, simply
to give up. Neither felt able. They were bound by politesse, sen-
timent, form. Tina felt a loyalty to the elderly man with whom
she'd once shared a pint of Tofutti ice cream. She felt a loyalty
to something less nameable besides. And yet, at the entrance to
the city archives, she hesitated. They both did. They stood on the
modest steps. They looked around. It was a mild morning. Weak
sun. Fog. In the street, a boy bounced a red ball through the gray.
Two others ran after him.

They heaved open the reluctant wooden doors.

The clerk had long since drafted a second, as in a duel. It exacerbated Tina's sense that they were falling, contra her company's every mantra, ever further into the past, into an era of telegrams and honor codes. She and the assistant flanked the desk, while Dave and the case officer continued their rhetorical maneuvers. The law was a matter of precedent, as he was no doubt aware. If the total value of the property in question was some thirty billion, and the treasury gave two hundred thousand to him, he who lacked the appropriate paperwork, who was to say tomorrow there wouldn't be a whole queue of Americans outside her door? Who was to say what would happen to her? It was worth lobbying the Germans to make good with everyone, including his grandfather, who, by the by, had not been home in years . . . The office acoustics seemed specifically designed to amplify outrage. The assistant kept her cool, took notes, transcribed and underlined her superior's what-ifs regarding Palestine. Multiple eavesdroppers scattered when they opened the door to depart.

The temperature had plummeted to unexpected lows.

On that last day, after the assistants scattered from the exit, after they were dismissed for the final time, they took a desultory trip to the famous Wieliczka salt mines. No bureaucrats. No papers. Just a deserted tourist destination at the end of the bus line. "Everyone recommends it," Tina said, defensive; it had been her suggestion, after all. Out the bus window, the world turned to fields and farms and auburn stalks partly buried in fallow snow. At the final stop, an obliging schoolgirl directed them up the dirt road to the visitor center, which served black forest cake and souvenirs. She was studying English, she told them. Exactly the kind of upstart, Tina resented herself for thinking, her firm had sent her out to find. They took two tickets, and the girl shrugged off a third. In the mine, aspiration blended with the dull glimmer of the walls. Had anyone ever seen so much salt? They considered a cart inert on its tracks. They considered an underground lake. They moved through the deep tunnels and into the belly of the pit to find a chapel carved entirely from sodium deposit: salt floors, salt statues, salt altar and chandeliers, a reproduction of *The Last Supper*, sculpted in salt relief. Salinity preserves everything. They thought of Lot's wife: don't look back. No wonder she never got a name.

Afterward, back in the bar with the same mountain cheese and blonde booths and waitresses, they watched a soccer game on her company phone. Neither of their teams were playing. Huddling together over the tiny screen, they clinked glasses whenever someone scored. Her boss's boss's messages kept interrupting.

"Persistent, huh?"

"I think I made a mistake."

The route back did not lead past the property. Nevertheless, they arrived. There it stood. An indifferent, five-story apartment block wedged between two others just the same, with stores at street level and dwellings above. The bounty of a bakery was glassed in, and bikes hemorrhaged from the racks and other available posts. At the entrance, a painted green door. The paint, the sills, the soft stucco of the façade, coordinated a pleasing if dilapidated tableau. The foreigners paused. With a toe, Dave gave the door an investigative nudge. To their surprise, it swung.

They mounted the pitch-black stairwell single file, searching the walls with their hands, waving arms at nonexistent sensors. Three flights up, they stopped. Counted the doors. It was the simplest thing in the world, it turned out, to find their way to the apartment. All the effort with the bureaucrats seemed suddenly so foolish. How much easier to just show up, ring the bell, ask for what's rightfully yours. It was a conversation two reasonable people should be able to have. There were no plans to evict anyone or raise the rent. Just the impulse to put certain things to rest. Dave knocked. Jiggled the handle. In that moment, Tina recalled the nights the historian used to break into her apartment and find her in bed; how she'd wake up with a hand on her neck; how certain things were not so easy to forget. Dave hesitated in his hope, his exhaustion, his grief, all of which seemed to be fraying his logical and locomotive functions. Then a child appeared. The boy hung from the doorknob by one small hand, so that his body contorted around the frame, leaving him at once inside the apartment and without. He asked something in Polish that they could not understand.

There are some experiences (threesomes, murders) that bind you profoundly if temporarily together, and whose effects are best worked off immediately in the name of regaining mutual independence—preferably over alcohol.

"I don't have any," Tina said. It sounded better than confessing to having finished it all.

His hotel was a ten-minute walk in the opposite direction from hers. "Christ," he said, in one fluid motion removing his scarf and flashing the key. They filed silently into the elevator. Upstairs, he collapsed onto the bed, shoes on, still in his overcoat. The lapels parted slightly to show the fly of his jeans. "Are these free?" she asked, opening the door to the minibar. "Doesn't matter." He reached out a hand, and she filled it with a vial. He studied it. "I hate this fucking country," he said. Then twisted the cap. What happened to whiskey? What happened to edible food?

Tina leaned against the foot of the bed with a shot of Baileys for herself. The TV flickered on. The default channel was the local news. She set to flipping through options in the sidebar menu.

"What are you looking for?"

"Porn."

"Sorry?"

"Kidding, kidding—they must have subtitles."

The empty vodka vial rolled across the duvet and settled against her thigh.

"You do you," he said.

Because it isn't up to you, is it? To say how other people ought to process grief. They watched the news without the subtitles. Dave's head was in her lap, and she stroked his hair. Oddly, she felt no spark; not in her groin, not in her heart, nor in the piercing that had caused them so much trouble once. They were too drained to feel anything at all. It was the desiccated exhaustion that followed a good long sob, though their eyes were dry. They talked on and off. The remains of the minibar were a pile of crystals between them.

The TV was still playing when she woke. Dave, still in his coat, was fast asleep. Her sweaty hand was in his curls. She extracted it. Through the windows, a quiet deep. She shifted him gently upwards on the bed, slipped a pillow under his head, then drew down the duvet. Removed his shoes. Opened his coat. The bottles tinkled. He stirred but didn't wake.

The moon paled the sheets and his worn-out complexion. She closed the door quietly, with a sense of relief, leaving the scene of a crime.

The final installment of the conference took place in a banquet hall on the ground floor of her hotel. No windows, no round tables. No bottled water, thank god. Just sound-absorbing curtains and rows and rows of folding chairs. The stage lights were bright enough to make her squint. Frankly, she could hardly open her eyes. After coffee, after spearing a pickle, after greeting all the acquaintances she'd supposedly made, and whose names it was unlike Tina to have so quickly forgotten, she took the microphone to introduce the concluding act. In the front row of the audience sat her boss's boss. Horribly, he winked. The speaker was an alumnus of the exchange program the company ran. Now very successful, of course. She praised his efforts and rustled up the perfunctory applause, then slipped to the side of the stage, into a half-conscious state, to respond associatively to the Rorschach marks of the former intern's slides.

On the projector screen, a little network of nodes appeared, linked by stick-figure lines. "The steps on a decision graph are binary and irreversible," he explained. "We call them directed-acyclic graphs. Or for short, DAGs." He'd latticed them with probability functions, then applied them to customer service platforms. Call waiting flowed through a course of open sesames, transferring customers from node to node. At each step, there was no turning back, and everyone arrived more quickly at their intended destination: a human voice on other end of the line. Where's my product? What's the deal? Why was I charged? "I'm just an engineer," the former intern said, earning a predictable laugh, "but they won't be complaining about wait times anymore." A few slides later, a simulation showed that the average wait was reduced by a whole minute per call. Tina was so startled by the applause she nearly lost her seat. She slipped a foot into a toppled heel and took back the mic. "Let's put our hands together for the power of the DAG," she said, realizing, with newfound gravity, how little she understood about the things she was paid to cheer on. She clapped awkwardly around the stem of the microphone. Her breasts shifted in her bra cups, irritating the wound.

It had become a real problem by the time she returned upstairs. She checked her phone. No missed calls. One shoulder hunched to relieve the pressure on her chest, she retreated to the bath. She'd spent too many hours in wool cardigans, in conferences, in salt mines, before returning to the cold. A buzz sounded. She glanced back into the room. The phone was on the duvet where she'd left it and the screen was black. There were fresh towels on the racks, and the sheets were turned down on the bed. A mint sat atop the pillow like a little foiled turd. In the palatial bathroom, she began to undress. She folded her jeans, her blouse, her sweater, nestled one bra cup into the next, and looked into the mirror. The usual disappointment. She pulled at her cheeks. Her brow. Turned chin upwards to inspect a zit, the kind that always appeared after nights of drinking in variable climes. Then she mixed a packet of saline in a paper cup. Rotated the piercing on its axis. A pearl of pus appeared. She ought to have removed this appendage long ago. Instead, she lowered herself into the saline. Her laptop was propped on the marble counter among the glasses and soaps and shower caps. There were emails to write. Follow-ups to send. All in all, she was very behind. It was high time. Instead, she scrolled. Searched her own search history for lists of citizens of Białystok and Radziłów. The daylight slipped away. The water in the cup grew cold.

In the morning, the carrion languished on the cobblestones, wires rising like new sprouts. Who loses a laptop in the street? Maybe it had fallen from the sky. The concierge observed it silently from his post at the revolving door.

What a waste, he thought.

The woman from 413 came down, coat open, hands lost in her hair.

"Any messages—?"

The concierge, tearing his eyes from the machine—maybe he could sell the parts?—looked at her and frowned.

"Wait, yes, here. Just the one."

RUMPEL

Small towns have always produced dreamers, daydreamers above all. As a child, and even into adulthood, I often imagined myself in crisis situations. Say the nuclear plant were to go on the fritz, or the particle accelerator, or a fire from the microchip factory to rip through town. I wondered: Would I be the first to respond?

The landscape is ripe for hypotheticals around here, so it's anyone's guess why we weren't more prepared. I can't help but feel we approached our demise with a certain solicitousness. Turned a blind eye, as it were. Corporate tax breaks fell like confetti from the windows of City Hall, the beneficiaries of which included the very particle accelerator, nuclear plant, and chip manufacturer that would later cause such chaos under the direction of @. In the end the industrial expansion was not so much the promised injection of adrenaline into the region's stagnant economic heart as the construction of an entirely parallel vascular system. One almost suspects there was never meant to be any overlap between our two worlds at all.

I don't think there was anything special about me. I lived alone. I spent my days mining data at Midwestern City Insurance (MCI), where I was responsible for screening claims. That time your reimbursement got denied, or your premiums were raised? That was probably me, I'm afraid. It was a job. Around the office, leadership was fond of joking that when it came to reputations for corporate malfeasance, banking and pharmaceuticals had provided the insurance sector with cover for so long; now we were shielding tech. As I refreshed my pings on my commute home (nothing new), gliding through Midwestern City on the self-driving bus, I thought to myself, Just you wait, they're coming for you, too. Only we weren't, were we? American Technologies (AT) did its thing. We did ours. We were coming for no one. We were coming for ourselves.

And I consider myself complicit. Once home, I stripped to briefs and dress socks and carried my laptop to the couch to put in a few good hours blanking out. Supine, I propped the keyboard on a foam stand impermeable to micro- and/or other-waves emanating from the hard drive, and which the internet had rudely informed my mother would shrivel my testicles to prunes. She'd sent the contraption with love. When we spoke, her worn face maximized on the same screen where I admit I occasionally watched porn, she'd ask, "Are you using it now? Are you? It's very important. This one study said the sperm count of men who—" *Click.* "Talk soon, Mom."

Picture me then, if you can bear it—splayed out, socks raised, belly rising yeastily over the castration-protection plinth, my ingress to the internet. My question is: Was I really such a threatening specimen? Or, for the sake of argument, do we simply observe a synecdoche for the nation's sad demise, an innocent if conspicuous conduit channeling late decadence the way a lightning rod conducts— Never mind. To complete the tableau, I dined on PB&Js from a salad plate, sometimes two in a row, because no one was there to judge. I'd shuttered the Venetian blinds. That the testicle-shield was upholstered in stretch nylon, absorbent of condiments of all kinds, struck me as a major design oversight.

This is to say that aside from work, my encounters with the wider world, and especially with women, took overwhelmingly the form of pre-recorded content. I'm not proud to admit it. But also, I suspect you're not surprised. I relay this information as a gesture of objectivity. I offer the facts, so that you may later decide if they are in any way exonerating. The women I watched were fully occupied across multiple orifices. I didn't see where I fit in. I didn't fit into my own life. When I was done I fell asleep, sometimes in bed, sometimes just like that, on the couch, in socks and briefs. End scene. Oh, spare us, Mother. What else did you think I was going to use the lap protector for?

It was around this time one began to hear of the irresistible charms of KINGDOM, the craze for which had only just begun. It's a wonder, in my fallen state, that I'd avoided it so long. People were calling it the game-changer of games. Other VR options could feel just as real, just as absorbing, perhaps even more so. What you heard about KINGDOM, however, was that it was more than just a virtual world. It was a tender welcome, a form of direct address. It spoke to you somehow. And it was terribly beautiful. Whereas other realms always betrayed the presence of underlying algorithms, tugging at your wallet, here the artifice was buried so deep, the sense of truth so overpowering, that the experience was said to approach the sublime. Users plugged in not to escape themselves, but to feel less alone. As a master of self-disgust, I assure you: the difference is profound.

Whatever relief it may have offered one's general sense of isolation, however, disappearing into KINGDOM was not without its costs. Quite literal costs, from an insurer's perspective. At work, I had the numbers. Addiction was on the rise, and with medically resonant consequences. The diagnosis codes pointed to a kind of schizophrenia, but as far as I could tell no one showed any improvement on the drugs we were obliged to reimburse. In my nonprofessional opinion, it seemed users had simply lost the ability to exit a parallel world, a hypothesis supported by my observations of the addicts who began to appear in the streets. They mimed everyday tasks, spoke in reveries to pleasant-seeming people who were not in fact there. At the supermarket, I caught a young man frozen before a bin of bananas. He was brushing his teeth, though there was no toothbrush, no toothpaste, no sink.

At home, Mom's face appeared on the screen. "Are you using it?"

I knew better than to share that, as far as I could tell, we faced a threat far more dangerous than those trained, ever so narrowly, on my testicles.

Suffice to say the only arena where I excelled was work. This may seem contradictory, lackluster as I was in nearly every other domain, but I was good at my job. I took pride in my ten years at MCI, whose competitive salary and benefits helped to secure my one-bedroom condo while also guaranteeing a mortgage for my mom. MCI is a legacy employer, the only local corporation not to have fled in the wake of AT's rise. It was enough to spark in me the faint, indulgent loyalty I imagine one might harbor for a distant relative. I'd like to think I'm not the only one who viewed the MCI mclogo with something resembling respect. I hoped it was mutual. In any case insurance seemed positively innocent compared to the chills I experienced whenever I passed an American Technologies sign: @. None of us really understood what @—under whose umbrella the laser, chip, and nuclear plants, not to mention the particle accelerator, had recently been agglomerated—was up to at the time. But KINGDOM was rapidly becoming its most popular product.

I've always had a knack for programming. Forgive me for boasting, but for reasons that will soon become clear, it is important to establish that in this narrow sense, I was not in fact your average cog. Insurance had taught me the central lesson of my life: everyone condescends the nerd, the dork, the chubster, until there's money involved. And the more money was at stake, the more brightly I shone. I was a steel trap. I sped up programs 2x. Executives passed on other associates' results to me to audit. A client-ready report, an analysis of adverse events incurred by patients on Drug Y versus Drug X, promised by next week, was filed the afternoon the request landed on my desk. They called me the Kingpin. Like in the video game. Which was what increasingly drove business. As users were becoming more hopelessly addicted, @ was establishing a pharma division to develop drugs to wean them off. (I believe this is what they call horizontal integration.)

My performance might have been a liability vis-à-vis my relationships with my colleagues, except that I had one other and irreproachable virtue in their eyes: I didn't want their jobs. A promotion had been offered early on, and, in a rare stroke of long-term strategic brilliance, I'd declined. From then on I was a nonissue as far as everyone else's ambitions were concerned. The associates, many of whom harbored highly unflattering memories of me from school, eased up when I rewrote their programs, helped them to get new jobs, secure promotions; soon enough, they became my boss. I was a market-maker, a company confluence. Every line of code passed across my desktop.

In standard internet forums, too, I was a star. I had nine lives and a reputation on populist crypto platforms. Thousands paid for subscriptions to my newsletter, in which I discussed the art of the short. Hundreds more logged in to watch me live-trade, as if markets were no more than a collective LARP, which . . . I wouldn't say they aren't. I toggled across various accounts on a timer, the way grand masters conduct multiple matches at once. Classic Réti Opening: knight to f3. I hacked, mined, and verified transactions on the blockchain. Bewildering mountains of virtual cash appeared, though it wasn't clear if it was liquid; wasn't clear if it existed; wasn't clear, if it did, if it would last the night. I didn't mind. I had no use for nice things. I sought only to exercise the full capacity of my intelligence, max out my human RAM. As long as I had an internet connection, I was the knight, the bishop, the queen, the Kingpin indeed; I owned the entire chessboard.

Offline has always been a different story, I'm afraid.

The year 20—, the same year of KINGDOM's release, found me shipwrecked on the island of my only relationship. Constantine! Two years, gone in an instant. "That's nothing," she said. "You have no idea what a relationship is." The worst part was, she wasn't wrong. It was a painful end. I delved ever deeper into MCI subroutines as well as into seedier, less mentionable pastimes. When I looked up again, it was just this past February, and crypto had risen astronomically. It appeared I'd made some two hundred and thirty million, enough to go in with a buddy, had I a buddy, on a small island off Dubai. All this time, I hadn't spent a single cent.

Not much of my decision-making up to this point had been about getting rich. But certain back-of-the-envelope calculations are unavoidable. I walked into the kitchen for a sandwich, which I consumed over the sink. Then to the couch. It occurred to me, Who needs a buddy? I was heartbroken and sick of my life. I'd buy half an island. Maybe I'd bring my mom. I rebooted my computer, navigated to my account—fuck the banks, they didn't deserve my money, why not?—and tested the log-in page, only to be met with a curious result.

All my life, I've been able to recite credit card numbers, customer accounts, chess sequences, social security numbers, and passwords that I should probably forget. Mom calls me for her debit and banking PINs, even though I've stressed we shouldn't be reviewing that kind of information on unsecured lines. Only as an occasional, anxious backup do I jot down financial ephemera. The self-driving bus might crash, for example, scrambling one's capacity for recall. It turns out that heartbreak is just as detrimental. Returning to my computer, I found that, like an unsolicited software update, emotional devastation had wiped my cookies clean. I retyped the key. Tried leaving it up to muscle memory.

Password not recognized

The extent of the problem began horribly to dawn on me. I tapped the side of the screen. My computer! How could it forget?

I was suddenly faced with the nearly impossible task of hacking my own account.

Locked out of my candy mountain, I backslid royally into humiliating routines. I looped in servers from the office to help churn the wishful SQL code I wrote to crack the key chains to my own mind. I stared at the program. It never progressed. When I did sleep, I dreamt of alt-me, Dubai me, Swiss Alps me, hopping from mountain chateau to mountain chateau, million-dollar accommodations that in retrospect borrowed embarrassingly from certain Hollywood movies. It wasn't only myself I mourned. Mother, my mother! I could have bought her a house. For years she'd nagged me about a knoll in Midwestern City's central cemetery, a grassy thumbprint in the earth nestled in the roots of a benevolent oak. I had planned to buy her that plot. I resolved to reserve it for her that very evening with whatever savings I had left. I'd buy her the whole cemetery, as soon as I recovered my crypto access. I straightened myself up and wiped my eyes. Found an apple and brewed a stale sachet of tea. Logged into my sorry fiat bank account. A plot was 10k, and I was at most half as liquid as that. I reviewed the available offerings, only to find my mother's chosen resting place had already been snagged.

It was the KINGDOM addicts who kept me from sinking into an even more irredeemable depression. They drifted through town as quiet warnings of what I might become. You spotted more and more of them now. On my way to work, they floated past the bus window in worlds of their own making, holding up foot traffic with tasks that seemed to be growing in scale. It was a dark sort of game, trying to guess what their miming meant. I observed a man lugging what appeared to be a long, heavy rope along the storefronts, or else a light rope attached to some burdensome cargo. Several more laid invisible bricks. One woman tried to do so in the middle of a crosswalk. We left her to her wails; from her perspective, I suppose we'd crashed brutally through her wall. They were going to get themselves killed, these addicts. Why did we tolerate it? Why didn't we take action then? I suppose there was a general sense that they'd done it to themselves. Privately, however, we were envious. To dissolve into a parallel life in a parallel world in which you were imbricated, progressing according to some inevitable plot of a flair and beauty Midwestern City was unlikely ever to achieve—well, our bus route paled considerably by comparison.

To keep from becoming another data point in my own spreadsheets, then, I resolved to a material program of self-improvement. I alighted from the bus two stops early and walked the rest of the way. For groceries, I settled for a sack of apples and obscenely priced boxes of jasmine tea, which were also obscenely fragrant. There was a nobility to standing in my ravaged kitchen, among the paper scraps, steeping floral antioxidants. Pulling myself together, I zinced up the bridge of my nose. I went out for walks.

Midwestern City, as you know, has a number of pleasant strolls. They planned miles of paths in advance of the Major Tournament we were supposed to host. The sprucing, repaving, the fresh cul-de-sacs topiaried and lampposted, had tunneled through the apartment block where I was born. The lake and ornamental canal were flanked by glass palaces that ran along the shores like endless mirrors: Who's the fairest? Not I. The new construction was occupied exclusively by @ folk, and one had the feeling they considered themselves benevolent for allowing the rest of us to remain. Everywhere you turned, you were reminded of all that you had never wanted until you, say, lost your crypto password. It was the aura of possibility that nagged.

A literal Aura, in fact: the shimmer first appeared by the glass chateaus on the canal, around the time of KINGDOM's rise. My own building was at the outskirts of this celestial glow, near a patch of trees. It was a temporary glade, earmarked for further luxury development, but just as they broke ground, someone had found the Aura and then—gasp!—a bird. All the real wildlife was by now protected in the actual Zoo, making this lone sparrow a miraculous vestige, one that had triggered the full force of the housing department's environmental codes. (They hadn't cared about the Aura.) The case was by now so red-taped at City Hall that those of us still living in the neighborhood had allowed ourselves to become attached to this rare parcel of green, chosen, after all, for its scenery. I often strolled here while listening to nature sounds. That my virtual fortune had ballooned to surpass a small and resource-rich nation's entire GDP was exactly the kind of thought on which I vowed not to fixate as I waded through downy grasses and silent pines, dew soaking through my cargos. Nevertheless,

I was comforted to think that the developers shared my pain. The glade taunted them with equal financial impoundment. With its idyllic pines and seas of grass, they could have easily charged three times what I paid for my own apartment, which looked out onto the bus lane. It's possible I was drawn here for the schadenfreude alone.

One morning, my earbuds died. There I was, damp to my knees with dew, listening to birds and insects and other kinds of wildlife one expects to appear in glades but which no longer do, and in the next moment, to actual silence. I took a step. It was eerie to experience the landscape sans the soundtrack that ought to have accompanied it. The totality of the silence—no traffic, no cars, no buses, no ambient streaming from neighboring phones, and above all no wildlife—made me truly if only temporarily forget my own misfortune. Well, shit, I thought. No more birds. That is genuinely tragic. I took a moment to honor their absence. Then I heard a faint little sound.

My heart raced. Could it be—? The lonely little scamp, I thought, to have single-wingedly stymied the developers! I slowed my breath. No breeze rustled in the pines. There was a mechanical quality to the song that struck me as extra-avian, a cross between a beatbox riff and a whistle—almost a religious chant. I scrambled up the knoll as quietly as a man like me can. Removing my earbuds, I leapt between patches of moss. I was a hunter, a scavenger, a survivor, I thought, more in touch with my corporeality than I had been in months of watching porn. Frankly, it turned me on. Which slowed me down. This here was experience. The earth and the man, the grass, the prey, the hunt—! Though in this scenario I was of course a savior. The chant grew louder. I was closing in.

A crop of ferns stood between me and a small clearing. I crouched behind it. Through the lace of the fiddleheads lay a patch of dirt and an odd little scene. A dancing man orbited a fire pit. He was elvish, not even half my height, accenting his syncopated hyperchatter with little jerks, manipulating his voice with the muffle of his hands. It took me a moment to decode the message. "001 1001!" he said.

My phone rang. It was my mother, a detail important only in that I had, like many children of parents a little too keen to be in touch, furnished her with a ringtone of her own, the better to screen her calls. It was a funeral dirge, in fact. As an accompaniment to the deranged elf's binary chant, also distinctly disharmonious. I cursed myself for forgoing the virtues of silent mode. But how was I to know? There was something almost digital about the glade. The silence of the supersaturated green recalled the dead zone of a VR space. That is to say it was not a place where you expected to receive calls. The green veritably ensured the absence of network coverage.

The interruption in any case was justifiably unwelcome. "001 1001!" said the imp. He sprang over the flames, heading in my general direction. Clutching the offending gadget, I dashed back down the path. He was a quick little imp, propelling himself in great bounds. I faked left, faked right, tried to lose him in the fiddleheads, which is how I found myself back in the clearing by the fire, running circles around it myself. If only I were doing this by joystick, I thought. Then I'd have the advantage. The creature, sensing that I was waning, pursued me with a demonic focus. He'd begun his chant again. "001 1001!" I regretted my PB&Js. I had half a mind to call my mother back, to tell her that I loved her and that this was the end. I was sorry I hadn't made better use of my talents or my sperm, that I had failed to reserve a resting place for her, alongside which she might now snag a spot for me. I reached for my phone. The imp dove for my ankles. I went down like a cartoon.

I couldn't tell you if what the imp said next was still in binary code. If it was, then I suppose it is a language I technically "speak," in the end. What I can offer, in any case, is the following transcript of what I heard:

"Who are you?"

"Nobody. Your neighbor. I work in insurance!"

"These are overlapping sets from which no unique solutions can be deduced."

"I'm harmless, truly!"

"Query 95 percent confidence interval for optimal descriptive category. Else, crack elbow."

My whole being concentrated into a single point, in particular, the vertex of my elbow joint.

"Depressed," I finally said, "with confidence 99.99 percent."

My hip-high opponent might not have seemed like such a formidable challenge, but I was pinned. What I would like to suggest is that he was not just a supernaturally strong but a supercomputing imp.

And he was pumping me for information. I must confess I wasn't always so calm under pressure as I am now. He turned circles on my back, securing first my arms, then my legs, then my arms again, as if I were a new device he was unsure how to turn off. Vague advice about power-to-weight ratios returned to me from my extremely limited time at the gym. It served only to confirm my disadvantage.

Cheek to dirt, a supercomputing knee stabbing into my lumbar, I admit I coughed up my woes, my despair.

I explained about my crypto.

At this confession, I was released. Crouching on his haunches in the ash we'd kicked up around the firepit, the imp fell into a deep consideration. I took the opportunity to gather myself into the fetal position on the forest floor.

He said, "I can calculate your password, but in return, you must give me your next girlfriend."

"Ha!" I replied. For obvious reasons.

The imp scuttled over to the fire and wrapped his arms around his knees. He gestured at his lonely board.

"I want someone to play chess with."

This is no bedtime tale. Nor a novella. We will proceed deductively from the available evidence. Nowhere did I grant the imp an answer in the affirmative. Neither did I explicitly refuse, that's also true. But I signed no papers, negotiated no terms, suggested no interest. Any reasonable person would infer from the tone of my response—I refer here to the *Ha!*—that the speaker in fact declined the imp's ridiculous and frankly misogynistic proposition to engage in hypothetical human trafficking. I had only just brushed the evidence of my defeat from my khakis and hurried back into the ferns when I heard him call a knight to f3. I remember thinking that he wanted *me* to play chess. And I was keen to cut our acquaintance short.

It wasn't until I reached my condo that I began to wonder how the imp had found his way into the lifeless woods. What even was he? I opened my phone to check for recent PSAs.

The Aura was the very reason, you might recall, that the Major Tournament for which our city had been selected host was suddenly canceled. All that sprucing up for naught. All those tax dollars down the drain. All because of this innocent shimmer over the canal. Of course the tourists wouldn't want to visit Midwestern City now. But what about us? For months, and despite the nonchalance of the housing department, anxiety had hung over the metropolis. People worried of a leak from the particle collider, where they were hard at work cooking up new worlds, discovering the origins of ours. But as City Hall soon announced, with no small help from our very own MCI, the Aura was an ultimately harmless, naturally occurring phenomenon. There was no measurable uptick in adverse events, at least none that could be observed somatically. And so we came to accept the Aura as a part of the scenery. Like the addicts, or the clouds.

In deeper internet dives, however, one found less benign hypotheses. This is always the case. You can find evidence of any and every theory on the internet. For example, semirespectable studies confirming that your laptop will prunify your balls. Message boards teem with recommendations for longevity that would have you hermetically sealed, blogs crop up to justify your every fetish. There are people who believe that *we*, you and I—that is, the entire population of Midwestern City—are in fact no more than a kind of testing ground for some other world more real than ours. In a similar vein, even back then you could find kooks who argued that the Aura was itself a kind of tear in the virtual fabric, propagated by the particle collider, and that through this breach a few programs still in beta had escaped into our world, such as the one that deleted all the birds. Public understanding remained that they'd simply migrated south; we're used to the idea, here in Midwestern City, that people would rather be somewhere else. But dark web chats suggested otherwise. It is our very obligingness, they said, our tendency to underestimate ourselves, that has allowed the Aura, and by extension @, to take such advantage of our town. I'd never believed in any of this myself. But that afternoon, following my humiliating scuff-up in the glade, as I rolled the crust of my third stress sandwich into a ball and popped it into my mouth,

I couldn't shake the feeling that the imp had had something of the Aura about him, too—a touch of something shimmery and slick. I recalled the staccato rhythm of his chant, the reverberations in my chest, how it was so very syncopated as to be random—not very melodic at all. I wondered if he weren't, in fact, a glitch.

First heartbroken, now paranoid—I shook my head. A good night's sleep can usually put such existential doubts to rest. Two pills and twelve hours later I woke up determined to forget the entire incident. I dressed for work, downed my orange juice, hovered over my laptop while brushing my teeth.

My crypto tragedy seemed far away; a brush with mortality puts things into perspective. It was out of sheer habit that I went to check the interim SQL progress. The screen was still asleep as I approached, the program whirring on the other side. Toothbrush in one hand, I touched the other to the trackpad. I knew to expect no change.

Only today, to my astonishment, a result had finally arrived.

The resolution sat there at the bottom of the log. I could have died with embarrassment.

i<3constantine

Hands trembling, I copied this humiliating reminder and navigated to my account. There were my Bitcoins! Which, sans supervision, and like a secret garden of incestuous quintuplets, had in my absence spawned.

How to describe my response? I admit of joy and its opposite. Who wouldn't welcome four hundred and twenty million to their name, regardless of plans to ever actually spend it? It occurred to me that with this kind of cash, I could easily evict the overachieving bidder from my mother's rightful grave. I was deeply proud of the success of my program.

And then immediately afraid. After all, the chances of success were so low that one had to reject the possibility outright. Statistically speaking, the success of my program veritably confirmed external intervention.

I was so terrified that on the way to work I missed my stop. At the office, I bungled the coffee machine. The cup overfloweth'd. "Silly you!" said Maria from HR. We analysts were so incapable in any and every unprogrammable task, it was part of our brand to flub domestic chores; she suspected not a thing. "Ha, ha," I said, as she hung the dishrag on the handle of the communal oven door. I was afraid, back in my cubicle, to turn on my computer. My programs were the means by which, I felt, the imp would hack my life. And so what would happen when I booted up for work? I didn't really want to know. Ridiculous, of course. I sat at my desk and bounced my knees. Snapped the blinds. Wiggled the mouse. Even if the Aura wasn't real—and I was still determined to believe it was not—I had the sick premonition that It wasn't done with me yet. I sat there in my chair with my hands folded on my desk. If I didn't reboot, the little icon beside my avatar would remain red in the office chat, and then everyone but Maria would think I hadn't shown up for work at all. My fingerprints hit the trackpad. I opened my eyes. For the retinal scan. The desktop loaded. Apps populated cheerfully, arranging themselves in categorical bins. Totally normal. I had fifteen new emails. Mom was cropped in the upper right corner of the screen, drinking a mocktail on the balcony. The bougainvillea heaved. "Morning, love," she said. "Running late?" I breathed a sigh of relief.

For a few blissful hours, I almost forgot how absurdly liquid I'd become (again), or that dark forces had fixed a target betwixt my sloping shoulders. I entertained modestly moneyed dreams: I'd buy my mother a house with a real yard, in which her bougainvillea could run freely. The man in his Swiss chateau, hypothetical me, stared into the amber residue at the bottom of his snifter, looking rather sorry. I banished him from my thoughts.

The model I'd been tasked with building that morning held my full attention. We were supposed to compare rates of success between Antipsychotic A and Antipsychotic B, both of which showed promising off-label potential for treating mass KINGDOM addiction. By now even the national news outlets had caught on. I didn't care so much, this morning, what the drug was for. I was simply glad it had nothing to do with me. By the time my program concluded, Antipsychotic B had pulled ahead: it brought KINGDOM addicts back to reality with an efficacy rate of 24 percent ($p \leq 0.05$) and a 10 percent lower incidence of nausea besides.

On the bus ride home, my levelheaded calm endured. I was pretty sure, for example, that I didn't really want an island off Dubai. I checked the markets. All indicators suggested that Bitcoin, like KINGDOM, was still on the up and up. Perhaps I ought to hold on? There was nothing I needed immediately, except of course to bribe the cemetery into selling me my mother's rightful grave. The idea brought tears to my eyes. It seemed the family name would end with me. I thought of the two of us there in the soft ground, decaying side by side. At home, I went to my desktop to divest one hundred grand in the name of my mother's eternal rest—plans for a proper mausoleum were taking shape in my mind. I copied my adolescent password from the SQL output and logged in to my account.

Next door, my neighbor was nailing something into place. The drywall shuddered. The dial on my computer spun. I waited for the transaction to complete. I still hadn't spent a cent. Not yet. The hammering next door grew louder and louder, like a drumroll. Still the dial spun. As the screen resolved, there came a strange, destructive screech, followed by a sudden storm of insulation that made it impossible to see. As the debris settled, I could make out a large hole opening onto the apartment adjacent to mine. Centered within it, a woman's dusty silhouette, the hammer still raised in her hand. The drywall dulled the dark luster of her hair like volcanic ash. It clung to her eyelashes, fuzzed her upper lip.

"Damn," she said. "My bad."

Though I may seem a coward and a swine, I believe in chivalry. For all my flubs, the greatest sorrow lies in not being able to protect the people I've loved. From KINGDOM. From myself. I ought to have told Clara then and there that I was cursed. That would have been the real act of passion.

Instead, mesmerized, I answered, "That's okay, I have insurance."

Clara, for her part, did not. I studied the gash she'd made between our two abodes. "Could I borrow your hammer?" She obliged. I drove a second nail through the wall, from my apartment into hers, conscious of her curiosity as I chipped away. It took a while, considerably worsening the mess. "There," I said, wiping my brow as the second plume began to clear. Now, when MCI came to investigate, they'd be able to confirm that it was I, not she, who'd caused the collapse, and my policy would cover it.

The home insurance division, however, did not share our sterling reputation. It was horribly backed up at the time. There were any number of overdue complaints, starting with the preparations for the Major Tournament and accelerating with the advent of the Aura, and claimants were facing significant delays. Clara and I were looking at months of living more or less as roommates. I tacked up a bedsheet. It was impossible to forget that she was on the other side.

More than any vow or diet or tea cleanse, it was the mere fact of Clara's presence that permanently revolutionized my routines. I couldn't possibly continue to indulge in salacious content with her nearby. I found myself listening for her movements. I became attached, I must say, to the rustle of her robe, the whistle of the kettle, the sound of her puttering about her morning vanity. I understand that I should not have listened, should not have projected the two of us together in her kitchenette, which I imagined (correctly, as I would later find) to be a mirror image of mine. I ought to have worn earplugs. But Clara is a woman of enormous charms, and I am a selfish man. "Hey," she said one morning, a week or two into our housing predicament. "Do you drink this shit?" She gave a little rap on the wall and then pulled away the sheet. A fist appeared, waving a box of green tea. Then the sheet lifted a little further, revealing the sharp line of her jaw and one of her eyes. We looked at each other; I from my dresser, struggling to fix my tie; she from the porthole, crouching slightly, the rest of her face still hidden behind the delicate floral pattern. (I'd used a sheet Mom bought.) Her soft fringe fell like sea-foam over her brow. She blew it aside with a little orca puff.

"I grabbed the wrong box at the store," she said. "And it was kind of expensive."

This became a morning ritual, jurors. We woke up. Clara would make two cups of tea, one green, one black, and pass the first through the hole in the wall. I was reminded it takes an audience to recognize that you exist, that you're still here. I wondered how long it was since Clara had really talked to someone about her life. For me, excepting video chats with Mom, the answer was, too long. Over tea, I told her about my break-up, my job. I confessed that I'd once struggled with an addiction to porn, though I might have located this misfortune in a more distant past than was strictly accurate. Clara raised an eyebrow, though she didn't scold.

"What kind then?"

I was in love.

I'd installed a little curtain hook to hold back the sheet so that we could more comfortably conduct these chats from either side of the gash in the drywall. With the curtain pulled aside, we sat each of us on a stage set solely for the other. Clara confessed she was divorced. I said that must have been hard. She shrugged. "He was a crazy fuck." She had a way of abruptly walking off whenever our conversations cut too close to the bone. We both had our secrets. After all, I hadn't told her about my crypto fortune. There was never time. The tea was drained to dregs. I had to leave for the office. From the depths of her apartment: "So long, sucker!" (Clara worked from home.)

She freelanced in game design but was also a wonderful analog artist. Her whole apartment was adorned with drafts of other worlds. I could see these partial murals through the threshold. They appeared as further portholes on cupboards, above baseboards. I asked her about them as we dined in the evenings, potluck style, passing dishes through the drywall. We never planned our menus out beforehand, but they always harmonized. Clara dipped a nugget into my boxed potato mash and brought it to her lovely mouth. She said of the murals, "They're helpful when I get stuck." She'd worked on the first two iterations of KINGDOM. A little ashamed, she explained that recently she'd been contracted for a reboot, which would launch next year. It was rumored to be even more real, all the more beautiful.

"Wow," I said, because I was genuinely impressed.

KINGDOM was the most popular game ever created. It was also the only game I ever feared, as I divulged to Clara that night.

I was concerned that I might lose myself among the addicts; after all, just look what had happened with me and porn. More than most, I was aware of the push to cover off-label applications of antipsychotics. One man had recently launched himself from the glass palaces by the canal while attempting a flying sequence. The consequences could not have been more serious.

"I hear it's the most aesthetically pleasing experience the world has ever had."

Her laugh was sad. "I guess." She popped another nugget into her bow-shaped mouth. "It depends on the person. I have nothing to do with the storytelling though. I'm strictly details. A flower here. A fungus there. Think trees that anticipate their own poetry." She invoiced for a cabbage, or Rapunzel, and engineers spliced it together on the backend. It was melancholic, she explained, to work so piecemeal on other people's worlds.

She worked very hard, Clara, that was clear enough. Though it was difficult not to feel it was a waste of her brilliance. Often she was still at it when I came home. I moved very quietly, so as not to disturb her flow.

"Do you know how to bootstrap an egghead shape?"

In the shower, I turned off the tap. "What?"

"HOW DO YOU BOOTSTRAP A—"

"Just a sec!"

Early on, we'd troubleshoot solutions through the porthole, the curtain secured demurely on its hook. Then, one evening, she invited me in. I bowed through the archway. Clara's apartment was just the same as mine, and yet another world entirely. Her windows looked on to the same drab stretch of bus lane, but somehow the room was unimaginably brighter, airier, the curtains billowing with a breeze that never graced my sills. She'd painted the kitchen mint green. There was a mixer on the counter, and a kettle, and a pot of violets. "Fake." Even still. I studied the ethereal murals on the walls. The bathroom was a disaster zone, the sink splattered with algae blooms of nail polish and mouthwash and shampoo. My heart swelled in my chest. I caressed her collection of perfumes.

"Which do you wear?"

"This one."

I took her hands, caressed her nails. "What color is that?"

"Carnivore."

After dark, we continued our courtship platonically, over the screen, via two-player games. We played GRIMMS and END OF THE WORLD. Clara was eight years younger than me, and so belonged to a different digital generation entirely. I showed her APOCALYPSE and INVASION; she introduced me to FARM. I was worried about losing her right from the start. I considered her a possible dream. In my nightmares, she dissolved into the sky and laughed in my face. We played, she in her bed and me in mine, the original version of LOOKING GLASS. She beat me every damn time.

Soon we were living out of both apartments. I quietly dropped the insurance claim. Neither of us wanted the wall boarded up now. After dinner, we sat together on my sofa and considered the gap. We had big dreams, Clara and I. We talked about tearing down the rest of the wall to let the special sunlight from her world spill into mine. Instead of hovering in the corner with her headphones, Clara could have the entire western front. "I'll build you the world's most wonderful desk," I said. I gestured to show her how it would run along the continental shelf of our united windowsills so she could work looking out onto the sunset. Clara did me the courtesy of imagining along, never pointing out that I was as hopeless with tools and analog construction projects as she was; that in fact the one time she'd asked me to install another hook on which to keep the shawl she wrapped around her when she entered my apartment, I had mangled the job. The hook was loose and askew. She would emerge through the portal, a little genie, and reach for the crooked scarf. (I kept the air conditioning on, Clara kept hers off, a collision of atmospheric fronts that kept our weather patterns aloft.) The only thing that stopped us, frankly, from pursuing further renovations was the very real possibility of crashing through the floor. That we'd have to pay for. Nevertheless, we continued to dream. Evenings, we curled up to watch the barrier that had formerly kept us apart as if it were a stunning piece of sky. We discussed the palace we'd create once we were rid of it for good. Then, one night, I took the joke a little too far.

"Fuck it," I said. "We'll buy the whole block." As a kind of afterthought, I added with a yawn, "Plus the glade out back."

We were on the sofa, sharing a bottle of wine. Clara's head was on my shoulder, and I was sleepy with the alcohol, and with her perfume, the hint of shampoo that always wafted from her fluffy hair. She was suddenly alert. Her hand clenched fiercely around mine, introducing the carnivorous nails that flew all day long across her keyboard.

"What did you say?" she asked.

"Oh, nothing."

"We could buy the whole building, that's what you said. What do you want with eighty apartments?"

"It was a joke!"

The shawl soared around her shoulders as she leapt from the couch. "It's people like you! Acquisitiveness! The origin of the evil at the center of the world!"

She disappeared. I stared at the naked hooks.

This was our first fight, jurors. Strong language had been used. I slept not so well. I clung to the record of our conversation, wondering where I'd gone wrong. I would never suggest that Clara was

133

prone to illogical or emotional flights, but I must admit that I was baffled. I turned onto my side and stared into the dark. I could feel her presence, like a second pulse, just a room away. Around dawn I must have dozed off. The gray silence woke me up. The old depression was there, hovering at the foot of my bed.

What do you do, a lover spurned, when the person you adore won't have you near her anymore? I got up and dressed for work. I was learning, jurors. I was at the mirror, sick yet stoic, clipping on my tie, when she crawled back through the hole in the wall with the two cups of tea. I rushed to relieve her of the mugs and help her through the passage, which still leaked silty streams of drywall every time we crossed. She elbowed me away, spilling Earl Grey onto the carpet. It was not her most elegant entrance.

She set the tea on the table with excessive force. "What did you mean about buying the building?" I might not have admitted it then, not in so many words, but I was so helplessly into Clara precisely because she was more intelligent than me. She missed nothing. In any case, she'd sniffed out the crypto fortune. And while I did not fully understand why my being so rich would cause such a rage—though it shouldn't have been hard to guess, given the behavior of the @ executives—I was of a mind to dispel her concerns as immediately as possible. I was no longer the figure with his snifter in the alpine chateau, however close I'd come. I'd left that man behind.

I was still strongly tempted to try to pass off my comment as a slip, but Clara was already snooping around my apartment for signs of unseemly spending. This was another thing I loved about my apparition. She wanted nothing to do with high-rolling men, nor with high-rolling people in general, the kind of person who lived in the glass towers along the canal. How could I explain to her that my once-illiquid fortune was as frozen as ever? I was powerless to spend another dime. Transacting the crypto for our family grave site had begun to seem the proverbial signature on the proverbial dotted line. And what I owed, should this completely unreasonable agreement come into effect, was the very woman standing before me now. I sat down on the couch. The loose tie dangled from my collar toward the floor. I hid my face in my hands.

"I have something to tell you."

I relayed the whole story from top to bottom, hesitating over but ultimately including the demands of the imp.

I was always aware that I did not deserve Clara's love. The morning I confessed my curse to her, I fully expected her to leave. Not just because of her disdain for profiteering, but because suggesting you believed the Aura was more than just some naturally occurring weather phenomenon was to be dismissed as a nut. The tea grew cold. Clara, perched on the couch, listened without interrupting. I'm losing her, I thought. She's gone. She took a sip. "I hate rich people more than anything."

She was hardly the only one. But Clara's dislike was more particular than it may sound. Her sister, she confessed, lived in one of those glass penthouses along the canal. Two of them, in fact. She'd joined them up.

"Admittedly, that was kind of our idea."

"That's not the point!" Clara seethed. Her nails flashed an updated shade of red. "She had something to do with that Aura, I know it."

It will hardly come as news that Clara's sister, Queenie, CEO of @, is one of the most powerful people in Midwestern City. She has since seized my property, had me fired from my job (to think how much I miss that cubicle now!), even threatened to seize my mother's grave site, which is really going too far. Leave the mothers out of it, I say. But no good ever came of dwelling on regrets. Let the record show that I am in no way accusing Queenie of criminal activity, as that would be slander. Instead, like a radio tower, I am merely and neutrally relaying information that was neutrally transmitted to me.

Clara paced the combined length of both of our apartments as she told her tale. Her fluffy hair, that perfect little pouf of fringe that she so habitually cleared from her brow, bounced with every step. She crossed her arms at the small of her back. Each time she met the ravaged wall, she stooped delicately through it.

"My sister and I are very different women," she began.

As Clara told it, they'd spent their childhood in the vicinity of the particle collider, acting out scenarios involving some version of "climb the fence." Clara was all dreams and engineering; Queenie a mastermind in leadership and rhetoric. She would have made a decent general, or a fine specimen of the aristocracy. Even back then, Clara said, she'd displayed a Machiavellian edge. A drawn-out divorce had put a strain on life at home, and so out they went toward the particle collider, to combine their dangerously complementary skill sets.

Once or twice a week, while their parents were meeting with the lawyers, Queenie would propose a proper visit to the heart of the plant. "They didn't give tours back then, not like today," Clara said. Her sister had asked her to devise a contraption that would help them clear the barricades. Clara assumed the challenge was to be pursued in the same spirit as the other games she and Queenie played, which is to say, as a kind of daydream. And what is a hypothetical, really, but a test of your capacities, a means of discovering where your limits lie? Clara devised sketches of the requested machine. It was only later that she realized she'd been purposely diverted. Absorbed in her highly theoretical designs, she hadn't realized that Queenie was simply memorizing the schedule for the changing of the guards, perched in a tree with her kid binoculars. "Come on," she said one night, taking Clara by the arm. They stole out of the woods, approached the fence, and slipped in behind an entering cart.

What first struck her, Clara told me, was the stillness. It recalled the glade by our apartments. She looked down at the grass. The particle collider lay just beneath her feet, and she wondered if she could detect the shimmer of its activities—a little tremor in the ground. She noticed the smell. That is, the absence of one. "I wasn't enjoying myself." The compound was characterized not by the electric charge of discovery, but the slick, withholding quiet of a cover-up. A premonition she'd learned to recognize from Queenie, no doubt.

Clara climbed back through the porthole and collapsed beside me on the couch. Now it was her turn to lower her face into her hands. I took her in my arms.

"She knew I wouldn't approve."

"Of what?"

Her forehead rocked against my shoulder as she shook her head. "It's all my fault!"

Clara looked at me with teary eyes. I held her close.

"Don't leave me," she said.

The particle accelerator, the imp, the confidential statistics stored in spreadsheets at MCI: assembling the various parts, Clara and I found ourselves in the unique and terrifying position of being the only people to understand the true predicament Midwestern City was in; Queenie had quite literal universe-building power at her command. The Aura was a breach in the analog and digital worlds, and we had begun to blur.

The one thing a program like KINGDOM cannot resist, jurors, is the proposition of a game. This is its only weakness: it likes to play. Assuming the temptation is proportional to sentience, then for a program as powerful as KINGDOM, giving in can occupy the better part of server capacity. We had some slight chance of hacking @ through the backdoor, then, if only we could design a suitably irresistible distraction. This Achilles' heel is not so different, really, from our own. We become obsessed by the pleasures placed just within our grasp, put up blinders in real time—and this is a surefire way to lose at chess.

After the city beautification drive demolished the apartment block where I grew up, Mom had appealed, like so many others, for relocation assistance. The process was slow, so slow that in the end we gave up and found a place ourselves, as the city had probably intended. The new co-op looked upsettingly like the old, so much so that I would think they'd simply relocated the original building, brick by brick, had I not watched the wrecking ball plow through it myself. In any case, Clara and I suddenly found ourselves in our own housing predicament. Our paradisical and partially conjoined apartments were no longer secure. Within the hour, we'd packed and boarded the bus for Mom's.

We rode in silence. The streets grew less familiar. Apartment blocks and offices gave way to greenhouse high-rises, and through the open levels spilt the little sprigs of snow peas and the deep verdant of artichokes, the evergreen rot of the rapunzel. Fecund tomato vines flailed over their containers like damsels in distress. (Clara whispered, "Let down your hair!") We got off at the end of the line, where a long, empty road led up the hill to the fortress where my mother now resided. The building stood as solitary as a watchtower at the crest. (This was useful for hiding out.) When the elevator regurgitated us out to 14E, Mom was already in the door, dressed for the calisthenics she always planned but rarely actually performed. A silk scarf secured her sporty ponytail. She held out her arms. "Hi, Mom," I said. "This is—" but already she was manhandling my face, as if she couldn't believe I was actually there. Her son, in real life. How rare! Clara, sensible as ever, took a diplomatic step back into the hall.

The nice thing about Mom was that she wasn't interested in why we'd come to stay. In fact, she seemed to intuit that we didn't want her to know. The first night, we let her dote on me. We loaded a game in the living room and tried to teach her to play. She couldn't beat a level to save her life. The mobs swarmed her every time. Nothing made her happier, it seemed. She sat between us on the couch and laughed and laughed.

"Aren't they cute!" she screamed.

Clara and I had been playing a lot of chess. What I had taken to be an intellectual union of the purest kind was in fact rigorous preparation. She'd been training us, I realized. We set up the board by the bougainvillea. This was the essence of our plan: instead of waiting for the imp to come to us, as we were certain that he would, we would go to him.

Clara paced around the balcony, balancing a bag of Cheetos in one hand. "My proposition will be that if I lose, I'll be his companion for life, playing board games or whatever. But if I win, he'll leave the city, and in particular the two of us, alone for good."

It was of course the former scenario that worried me. A neon sheen of cheese dusted her bangs. She trumpeted it away per usual. Her eyes narrowed as they always did when she was concentrating.

"While the imp and I are engaged, the rest of the network will get pretty distracted. That's where you come in."

I shook my head. Backlit by the bougainvillea, she glowed.

"You made four hundred million mining crypto," she said, as if my primary objection was the difficulty of the task. "You'll find a way."

The nightly dinner call came from the kitchen.

"Mac and cheese!" Mom said.

We spent two blissful weeks like this. For brief moments, it was even possible to forget our conundrum. To begin to imagine what it might mean to live a normal life together, minus the fact that we were living with my mom. She served us iced tea and went to the store. "Look at you! Always working," she said, so happy it seemed she might cry. She baked fresh bread and gave us the heels. We raised the buttered slices to our chins. Fresh steam rose through our plans.

"This is really fucking good," Clara said.

Inevitably, the conversation drifted on to less pleasant things.

"Dude, it was probably my sister all along."

It was during one such reflective moment that we heard an ominous thump. I slowly lowered the laptop lid. Clara retracted her legs from my thighs. Even the bougainvillea shivered. Quietly, we made our way to the door. Pressed an ear each to the surface. Clara's eyes were wide. Sure enough, we could hear the telltale signs. "oo1 1oo1!" The creature simply couldn't help itself. It was out there whispering furiously, even as it sought stealth. Clara brought a finger to her lips. With the other hand, she counted down. On the third beat, she cracked the door and then immediately slammed it again. There was a streak of light, followed by a crash. An imp-shaped hole had appeared in the door. Beyond, the ravaged bougainvillea. Its plundered pink vestments lay in ribbons all around.

·

Why, you might ask, would @, parent company of KINGDOM, put such effort into tracking Clara down? I wouldn't insult your intelligence with such an obviously rhetorical question if it weren't important. This being the only surviving testimony, it is imperative for us to dot every possible *i*, cross every *t*. And so dot and cross we shall. Who do you think coordinates your nondairy creamer with the xanthan gum that makes it taste so much like the milk that it is not? Who mines the tin for the peel-back tops of both your yogurt and your toothpaste, packaged to ensure that customers always use just a bit too much? That's right. I suspect @ even had a hand in those artificial islands off Dubai. And where to go for further growth, jurors, when you have already saturated the entire globe? To where does one expand? Nowhere. So one simply doubles the world. Starts over again. It was, in the end, a really quite elegant solution. And we were just a draft.

This is to say, jurors, that I believe Clara must already have had most of her plan in place by the time I confessed to her my idiotic and nonconsensual nonpromise to the imp. She was our savior from the start. Or, from @'s point of view, the last line of defense against our imminent deletion. I wonder now, however much it pains me to say this, if I was simply a means to her heroic ends. That's all. But my feelings aside, she sprang so admirably to action.

We returned to our conjoined apartments that very night and set up our desks on either side of Clara's porthole. Over the tops of our monitors, we each confirmed the other was still there. The blue glow of the screen fell over Clara's skin: she was in. I rustled my fortune and converted it all to cash. Clara brought out a box of snacks. I wish I'd paused to appreciate the way the late sun fell across her shoulders, her collarbone, how it brought out the highlight of flavor dust that hovered there, deposited as she rearranged a bra strap. She was golden. She always was. I rallied my old mining buddies from dark corners around the web. *Comrades*, I typed. *This is not a drill.* KINGDOM would wrest no more from our city, there would be no need to take Drug X or Y, no more cures for people whom @ was phasing out. *Comrades*, I announced into the chat again. I felt positively Shakespearean. I was Henry V at Agincourt, except no one was about to die. At least I didn't think so. *Comrades*, I typed once more, because, well, anaphora.

> *But if it be a sin to covet honour,*
> *I am the most offending soul alive.*

.

I myself have rarely played KINGDOM, jurors. But there is a scene, I recall, from Clara's piecemeal work on Level 81, when Rapunzel finally lets down her hair. You're standing there at the bottom of a tower, totally alone in the foreground of the scene, kind of hopping back and forth from foot to foot in that little dance avatars do when they're at rest and still trying to figure out the rules. Toggle right. Then a little left. All at once, the game decides. The hair drops like a guillotine. And spills and spills. The whole world is quiet. No woodland creatures interrupt your thoughts. And you think you're supposed to save her, you see. Like in the story. That's the only way to get out of this mess. To find the woman to whom all this hair is attached. Only the hair is monstrous. It floods the ground, encircles the tower like a moat. You do what you can. You start to hack away, only to find that it grows back twice as fast. So you start to climb, hand over hand, only the hair keeps pouring down, keeps growing, it's actually lowering you back to earth. It will be the end of you, this flood of hair. And look at you, you idiot, you walked right into the trap. In a panic, you start to slash. You use the machete you won levels ago. The blade shatters in your hand and falls, presaging your imminent demise. You're not thinking about the girl anymore. It's clear now you both have lost. You'd like to stop, but the game goes on. That's how it works, this level of the KINGDOM. There is no death. Just the slow, infinite catastrophe of drowning in royal locks. You can see your vitals start to drop at the bottom of the screen. But however much you struggle, tapping frantically at the controls, still the downfall, your downfall, refuses to bottom out. You're still thrashing. Still alive. The game continues even after you've given up, released the keys. Hair pours ceaselessly across the screen. The game will run for days or weeks like this, for as long as the power still flows. You realize then that you're just a lone organism battling its own exhaustion. The only way to exit is to get up, cross the room, and jam the power button—that is, if you can, to end yourself.

LETTER TO THE SENATOR

It was two in the morning and everyone was in Eileen's kitchen, of course. It was the most inspiring kitchen we knew. Lots of plants, shiny floors—she bleached the baseboards herself. There was a bathtub between the window and the oven that got a surprising amount of use during her soirees. Get clean, we recommended, whenever two of us were at odds. Go get clean in the tub. The pair popped in and had a heart-to-heart. She was a real homemaker, Eileen. We teased her for it, though we shouldn't have. What we could not see then was that people loved this about Eileen, *we* loved this about Eileen, her way with mopping up a floor and turning down a bed. It made us feel there was still a right way of doing things. Not that she was without a kink. I once heard she used an apple to—but never mind about that.

The idea of the letter had arrived an hour earlier, when it became clear that everyone was already writing to the senator in private. So there was a lot of material to begin with. These were crazy times. People started pooling notes. "Hey," said Sam. "What's this doing here?" He drew from his jeans pocket a single slice of processed cheese and added it to the pile. In the end everyone had something to contribute to the cause. The mound of grievances, propositions, three-point solutions, treatises, and Marshall Plans grew higher and higher as thoughts continued to emerge from the folds of our clothes, wallets, backpacks, engulfing the single peony in its vase.

The porcelain cracked. Eileen twitched. The papers scattered like the trash that, just a moment ago, they'd been.

We'd all had a few drinks by then. Still, it was clear the immediate task was to combine our critiques into a single missive. You can imagine the consternation this caused. A dual citizen recommended we try the groupthink of a Ouija. Great idea! Only no one had a board. Meanwhile Eileen and Jamal were in the bath, clothes on, bone-dry, having a heart-to-heart. Who knows what had sent them into the tub, but now their foreheads were an inch apart. ("So to deep clean the machine, you want white vinegar and baking soda, first the one, then the other," Eileen was saying. "Pour the vinegar into the detergent cartridge, then add a dash of bleach . . .") I looked at my friends. They were so familiar the whole kitchen seemed to blur. I found I couldn't remember their names. I sat at the table to collect myself. The stack of grievances loomed. I drew them toward me, plus the single peony to boot.

It's possible no one noticed me there, sifting through the drafts. I'm neither an influencer nor a writer nor an analyst, teacher, lawyer, not really gainfully employed in any taxable way—I slip through the cracks. Once I worked as a bank teller, but the customers barely noticed I was there. I'm hardly ever here, you see. I have only the one skill, really, besides moonlighting as the presence of myself, and that is that I can rewrite anything to make it seem profound. Oh, not my own ideas! It's not like that. At nine, after work, sitting on the high stool by the window in my room, craning my neck for a glimpse of the sky, I sometimes think of jotting down a note or two for a story of my own. But I never do. At the end of the day I'm so exhausted it's all I can manage to perch on the stool or lie in bed, let two slices of rye go stale on a plate—it's no real loss. That's all toast is, when you do not have a toaster: stale bread. Other people's ideas are no problem, however. I write them up with no trouble at all—I hate to see *other* people's ideas go to waste. I've been known to steal scraps from bus bins at self-serve restaurants, salvage term papers from the trash. In our school days nearly everyone in the kitchen had at one time or another rung me up with a request, Hey, could you read this? Of course! Though I wonder how it is they thought to call. I rise, perhaps, like a Loch Ness monster from the lake of the past in the vulnerable moments before they go to sleep. Oh, they must think, she's not so bad . . . and not so busy . . . Except for Eileen. The odd one out. She's the only one who never calls. (". . . set the dial to presoak," she advised Jamal. "That's when you add the bleach . . .")

From the table, I could overhear the many sides of ongoing debates. A high school teacher brought everything back to Homer. (He taught geography.) "The letter ought to be an epic," he said. "That's the new generation: Ulysses, exiled from a home rendered unrecognizable and trying to make his way back . . . So difficult to escape precedent!" Once, at a party I was able to attend only because no one noticed I was there, I caught a famous novelist by the wrist. "Hey," I said. "I read your stuff. Do you like Thomas Mann?" Indeed he did like Thomas Mann, whose influence I had detected in the opening pages of his book. I told him that, the way I saw it, narrators come in two types, on long leashes or short, and that at Mann's sanatorium the leash was decidedly—"I prefer his brother," the living novelist said. To think what a friendship we could have had.

Anxieties of influence! In the drafts before me I could detect traces of news anchors, talk show hosts, an article I'd read recently in an obscure online review, and also lots of Tolstoy, who for good reason is best remembered as a novelist and not a pamphleteer: *With the rise of automation, what to do with the poor?* (But the robots were coming for his job, too.) The most common complaint, however, once each letter was reduced to its essence, was that no one could tell what was good, what was bad, what was wrong anymore. What we needed, I thought, were magical mountains and dreams and a nice long leash, so that we might roam further from the nexus of our private fears and into obliterating wildernesses of snow. What we needed was a hint of ammonia or bleach to clear the neglected plumbing of our souls. What I wanted, I think, in some private corner of my mind, was for Eileen to see that I was here. I set to work.

Though I may seem a lonely person, there have been periods when I've known love. When I belonged to a pair, to a certain side of the bed, and never slept alone. When I was the spirit of the age. I went to sleep open to possibility, and in the morning my bedfellows rolled across me and stumbled out the door for coffee, not noticing I was still there. They called two, three, ten years later. "Hey," they said, as surprised as I was to be speaking on the phone. Our voices had deepened, richened, transformed. "How are you?" That's all writing really is. Obsession punctuated by long periods of forgetting. An attempt to capture the attention of someone you love. But what do I know.

I copped a line from the back of a napkin. Borrowed a paragraph on regressive taxation, an abstract about solar batteries typed up on an Olivetti. I added a dash of ethos. "No one is as naturally heedless and ignorant as we! All the more reason," I continued, "to take seriously our present level of concern." I was on a roll. The art of persuasion. I could feel the tension. The letter was coagulating into something dense enough to resist a lie. I told myself it was for everyone, though in retrospect I can see it was mostly for Eileen. I was entering a new reality, one for people like me, for whom ordinary phenomena morph into fantastical things. As a child, I went through a phase in which I could not stop watching *Fantasia* on VHS. I saw it nearly forty times. I fell very ill with the flu in front of the television and a 32 oz. bottle of ginger ale, and when I recovered, my outlook on the world had changed. I was still human, but I saw things less and less in agreement with the consensus view. At Eileen's, I remembered the swells of the sea, and the cliffs, and the white flowers floating in the water, so much water, those fairy-tale flowers came alive. I felt the great beauty of the inanimate world and knew it was a friend. The dark swirls of the music crescendoed in my heart. I wrote, "We are reaching a mythical end." I could feel something great transpiring in the war-wake of my ballpoint pen. I could sense the admiration of Eileen, her presence in the bath. I tore the papers, pasted, connected with arrows disjointed passages to direct the reader to forthcoming revelations. Someone turned the music on, turned it off, voices rose with angry joy. They were merging, humming, and meant to be heard. I was writing, I was scribbling, I felt a little mad. I have never felt more solid, I think, than when composing letters not my own. On behalf of the group. On behalf of someone I loved. I imagined *Fantasia*'s little Mickey in his star-spangled conductor's suit, rallying the waves. The hem of his cape fluttered over the cliff. I was focused on conducting the roiling ocean of a rapidly evaporating rage. Years from now, I used to think, what will they say about us? Now I felt I knew. This was all they'd need. I came to the end of the senator's letter with the same silvery satisfaction of sinking a knife into a fish. Then I folded myself up as neatly as I could and slithered through a crack in the floor, into the dark, into a world half an inch removed from here, in what I admit was only a partially voluntary turn of events.

Peering up through the small gap in the floorboards at the world of light I'd left behind, I allowed myself a little disappointed sigh.

After I fell through the floorboards, Eileen got out of the tub. She'd finished her laundry how-to with Jamal, who also emerged, a little dazed and in love. "Why so serious all of a sudden?" she chided her guests. What was this mess we'd made? She laughed, carefree, as she gathered the grievance scraps. People sheepishly reclaimed their thoughts, plucking papers from her arms. "Eileen," the narrative poet and teacher said, "we're trying to—" She glided across the room, righted the vase, gathered the ravaged peony. She was a real tableau, arranging the single flower in the chipped and clouded glass. The narrow mouth pursed around the slender stem. Her hair tumbled over a shoulder as she tilted toward the blossom with motherly concern. In her arm she cradled the remainder of the grievances, the ones no one had claimed. The room quieted. The moon glinted off the white gloss of the fridge. Eileen reached out a hand to plump the heavy peony bloom, and a few petals flurried away—I knew because the soft flake of one settled in the floorboards, near my nose. The narrative poet was the only one still going, still speaking, but mostly to himself. Eileen went to the closet and commenced with keeping house. She removed the broom, the mop. The red plastic bucket overflowed with suds. A kind of seance settled as she began to clean. There was nothing but the soft swish of the broom against the floor. At some point, she started to hum. I couldn't tell what, but the low tune cast a spell. On her knees, still humming, she polished the wide floorboards with a soft-bristle brush. Small storms of flour settled in a dustpan. She sifted it into the trash. She dunked a rag into the bucket and began to scrub. The shadows in her shoulders engaged around the sinews of her upper arms. I felt the water slosh in my ears each time she passed. I rubbed my eyes. I had a good view of Eileen through my crack in the floorboards. I no longer felt so far from home. There was no more talk of writing letters in that room where people slumped on tables, chins in hands. One by one, they fell asleep. The last holdout was Sam.

Try to narrate anything else, anyone else, make the moral disappear through a gap in the floor, and still it will reappear, if only in its absence. Through the slats, I glimpsed Eileen's face, beatific as she worked her rag across the floor, heading for the tub. I tried to follow, I had to follow. I crawled after her with the roaches and the mice to where she knelt. Then I got tired and closed my eyes. We dreamt along to Eileen's humming as she bleached away our fears. As we did, she undressed and stepped into the bath. If you want to know who someone really is, just see how she acts when she thinks she's alone. Though you won't ever get the chance. I've kept her for myself.

DUCK, DUCK,
ORANGE JUICE

The man I am driving to interview does not belong to the college, though he lives not so far away. I am to ask him about the upcoming election cycle. Perhaps I will. I promise out loud to myself in the car, *I will ask him his opinion in passing.* I say, *I will stay on task.* The car is old but fresh and belongs to my friend. The bumper stickers have opinions: on peace, on love. I think of the home she must come from. The friend, that is. Bottles of beauty products. The pictures on the mantel. A whole chicken will be marinating in the fridge, quartered lemons glowing in the gullet. The closets—very clean. I look into her rooms. I caress the dresses in the closets. Then look away. At the road. Through the pines, where a peloton of cyclists has blocked the lane ahead. I decelerate. I continue at a crawl. At this rate the guitarist will be asleep by the time I arrive. Then there won't be time for any interviews at all.

My friend has left her CDs in the CD player. A woman belts her sorrows from the speakers on the dash. I do not know the words. Even if I did I wouldn't sing along. I prefer a song without words, songs that don't remind me how difficult other people can be—songs like the guitarist's songs. They filled the rooms of my childhood. My father played them. I can't say I liked my father, but I liked the music he played—it was the music that drowned him out. I hid beneath the sofa and bathed my brain. I listened

151

for hours, studying the notes, studying upholstery, studying the sound of my father's staccato footsteps in the other room. The matted underbelly of the sofa was a loose sheet that exhaled like a sigh. I closed my eyes. On the guitarist's albums there are no complaints and no refrains, only the blue twang of the six strings, nothing more, though sometimes a violinist or a cellist joins. To me his music sounds the same way these trees look as the road tunnels through them, a shifting sheet of pine with more needles falling, inevitably, to the forest floor. The road tunnels. The trees shift and sigh. I turn off the music that belongs to my friend.

The address to the guitarist's recording studio can be found on the back of the CD. The cover art displays a red barn that looks very much like the ones you see in the valley around the college, situated in fields of yellow-green hay. The mountain range in the background behind the barn is likewise familiar—it is the cover art, frankly, that made me think to turn to the information on the back to see if the musician might live close by. He records in a second valley on the other side of the mountain range, in a town similar to the one where I am studying except that it does not host a college. The road runs over the mountain range separating our two towns, one with a college, one without. On the descent the road is rougher. The hayfields are yellower. The bloated barns bend more in the middle than do the barns around the college. I have often imagined traveling through the cover art and into the scene that it depicts, and now here I am.

I've never been to a recording studio before, but when I arrive it does not look at all what I imagined. I am surprised. Or rather, I am surprised I had such strong expectations for how a recording studio should look. I imagined a low and technical building with revolving doors and a receptionist, a bowl of mints in the lobby. What I find is a single-story house set deep in the trees and a garden and a white splash of gravel where with difficulty I park the borrowed car. A man in the garden stands surrounded by the blanched lumps of butternut squash and pumpkins, lifting large flat stones. The stones are for a wall he is building around the squash. He wears a flannel shirt and work pants, and his porkchop-style beard is gray. There is no picture of the guitarist on the CD insert, and I realize that all this time I had imagined him as having no face, nothing but a sound and a vague presence within it, the way a house set far back from the road suggests itself among the density of trees. I am suddenly nervous. There is an impulse to return to the car and drive away. Then the man looks up, alarmed. I have been spotted. I am a doe in the trees. He raises a garden-gloved hand. And there is no use in turning back, I think, after someone has shifted the weight of a small boulder beneath his arm in order to grant you a neighborly wave.

Still I feel like an intruder as I walk along the garden path. The dirt and small stones grind. When I ask the gardener if he knows the recording studio I am looking for he says, "But it's here!" The guitarist? That is he! He sets down his stone and the wall grows taller. And who am I? I am here to interview him for an assignment, I say, adding, for persuasion's sake, that I have been listening to his CDs for years. "I love your music," I say. The guitarist's face opens with surprise. Am I sure I have not confused him with someone else? "Quite sure," I say. And then I describe in detail the CD cover art, for proof. The expression on the guitarist's face is that of some-one confronted by a person he has not seen for many years, though we have never met. Then he invites me in for a glass of orange juice.

Over orange juice we take a tour of his home that is also a recording studio. In the part that is a house there is one coat on the hook and one bowl in the sink and one spoon and one book and one chair in the living room and one toothbrush in the bath and in the bedroom a single bed that is much too narrow for two. The pictures, framed and fixed to the bare wooden walls, are populated. I glance into the faces as I follow the guitarist across the room. We reach a door. Here the house ends, and the recording studio begins.

We pass through a widow's walk and into a separate, smaller structure that the guitarist explains was once a shed, and where there is a woodstove with a crooked chimney and vinyls without sleeves and one guitar and one violin and the enormous menace of a table saw used to build the widow's walk, the guitarist explains, when the toolshed was converted into a studio for the purpose of music-making. It still seems dual-purpose to me: garden shears the size of machetes hang from nails on the wall. I think about all the other things the guitarist might have built but hasn't. I imagine the part of the house that is a home filling with chairs and credenzas and soap boxes for holding magazines once the reader is through; there's no more news, the news is old and yet cannot be thrown away, it must be saved, in the event that someday it becomes relevant again. The chairs arrange themselves around the fire. I imagine all the people who might fill the freshly planed and sanded seats. They step down from the pictures on the walls. They sit, demure. Sipping orange juice. No one says a word. The burden is crippling. We are all of us waiting for someone to speak, but no one knows what to say.

The walls are chipboard, and inside it is cold. The wires of a looper pedal loop around the floor. I ask the guitarist how it works and he explains. He lifts the violin, attaches the wires, and lets an arpeggio resound, resound, resound. Then the pedal clicks, and a whole octave withers. The silence brings with it a revelation, as the number of members in the band as I had imagined it reduces from three to two to one: the guitarist is all three members in a single man. It had never occurred to me to think that an artist might play more than one instrument per track, though of course he can. It is by no means unheard-of. In fact, it is increasingly the norm to be one's own band.

"I suppose so," the guitarist says.

The guitarist—or the musician, rather, as he plays the cello and viola in addition to the guitar—is not famous. As we retreat from the studio and into the house, he tells me that when you play the sort of music he does, you don't expect to have fans. No one has ever considered him famous before, he says, not even himself, so please excuse his earlier surprise. Over a second glass of orange juice it occurs to me that I am the only person for whom the musician is famous. I am a fan. Quite possibly, I think, the only one. Driving hours to the recording studio to ask what he thinks about music and life and the dynamics of the band (if he would call himself plus the three instruments he plays a band) will be an unprecedented expression of fandom. I am a superlative. I take out my notepad to write down what I have learned. *Fans. Superlatives.* There I find a note about the other questions I had planned to ask.

Inspiration?

The musician looks at me with tired eyebrows, tired eyes. I would like to know more, I say, about where his music comes from, about what it feels like to be a band unto oneself. The musician sighs. "Well," he says. He rests his orange juice tumbler on a knee. "When I was your age, I made music to impress people. Then, when I was older, I made music because I was in love—I wanted to impress my wife. And now?" He sighs again. "Now I don't make much music anymore, and when I do it's honestly just to fill the extra time." The musician sips the orange juice, looks out the window. "That's not to say I don't feel the impulse. I have a . . . a . . ." He gathers his fingertips into a beak at his breastbone and then extends his arm, blooming his fingers as he goes. It is the pose a soprano strikes to steady herself through a sustained and challenging note, only the musician is silent, and we are not in an opera house but a bare wooden cottage with family pictures on the walls. He drops his arm. His body becomes loose and lazy inside his flannel shirt. "Anyway," he says. "I still feel the *impulse* to create." I nod. I wait through a respectful pause. Then I ask him who all the people in these pictures are, where his wife is now.

The musician is not famous, self-described or otherwise.
The musician is divorced.

He tells me he has a daughter who now lives with her mother, who today lives with a paraplegic in a house specially designed to zip him and his wheelchair up and down the stairs. The musician's ex-wife is a physical therapist, and the paraplegic a former patient. She helped to exercise the stiffness from his unmoving legs and to maintain mobility in his two arthritic arms that he now uses to reach for her at night, or to press the button at the landing that allows him to glide, still seated, up the steps. The irony, of course, is that the musician has two good legs and two good arms, not one of which is welcome to advance in his ex-wife's direction. He misses his daughter. She's also in college, like me, although at a different school much farther away. Also far from her mother. She has chosen someplace far from them both. When she goes home for the summer holiday, however, or on those days when campus is closed, and the college gently suggests that it is time to go home for a while, then the musician's daughter chooses to return to her mother's house, attractive for its being slightly nearer to her college and for the chair-elevators that glide soundlessly along the banisters. The musician says that no one comes to visit him anymore. He says this with a large, self-deprecating smile. No one comes by, no one visits. "I am old, I haven't," he says, "had a trick-or-treater in years." He maintains the smile as he speaks, although I rather wish he wouldn't. I never imagined the musician to be such a sad man, but sitting here in his living room in the single chair—he has taken the footstool for himself—I realize that of course it makes perfect sense. Those songs were always sad with shifting centers, the way that fields tall with hay wave and tangle themselves in wind, and have no center. I observe, out loud, that the musician's house is set back quite a way from the road, it's likely that trick-or-treaters are too economical these days to visit a house set at such a distance into the woods. "Kids have become very strategic," I say. The musician glugs the remainder of his orange juice. He looks to the muddied toes of his gardening boots. He has thought about getting an apartment in town, he says, perhaps above the shoe repair shop and within walking distance of the library. But then where would he garden, and where would he record? Above the shoe repair shop he would have to play very quietly or else face the repairman's complaints. I tell him that I, for one, would be glad to live below the musician's recording studio and listen to him record. Then I review my notes.

The musician is not famous, neither in his own mind nor otherwise.
The musician is divorced.
The musician prefers fun-sized to candy corn, but on the 31st buys both.

When the musician goes to pour a third round of orange juice I can see that he is not going to ask me to leave. He may never ask me to leave. Nor will he ask me to stay. And so I could stay, effectively. As long as I do not try to go. I listen to the sound of the glasses being set, the juice being poured. He takes his time. Alone in the living room, I try to imagine the two of us living here, together, in this home with only one of everything. Perhaps we could take turns. The chair is cushioned and set close to the fire,

I'm sure that I could sleep comfortably right here, on nights when the musician takes the bed. I imagine the first thing I would do, the changes I would make, if I were to stay. I'd hang some cheerful pictures, paintings of landscapes or people who have not left the musician behind. Perhaps I'd hang some drapes, the light lace kind with eyelet hems, nightgowns for a windowpane. Perhaps I would persuade the daughter to come home for a visit. Yes, that's what I'd do. I imagine her as only a few years younger than me, but less mature, such that the years between us are exaggerated. They show. She will come home and I will ask her about her midterms and tests and demand she do her homework. Derivations unfurl across the kitchen table. I remind her that you can divide through by xy only if every term has one of each, an x, a y, which is also why partial fraction decomposition can come in handy, otherwise you may never be able to isolate the variable of interest in order to derive its speed and acceleration, or else its position, if speed is the variable you've started with and the idea is to take the integral instead of the derivative. That's one thing I can hold over wonderful daughters like her—at least I am not stupid. Once she has relaxed, perhaps I will make pancakes. Measuring out more batter, I take a serious tone. I ask her, Really, how are things at home? *I am home*, the daughter says with a frown. I ask her what she thinks about the election cycle and find that she is pessimistic. *They're both screwy, we're all screwed.* I'm exhausted by the way she flaunts her breasts, but what can I say? That she must vote. That it would mean so much to her father if she visited more often. *How about your father?* she says.

The musician walks me to the car still holding our empty orange juice glasses. He carries one in each outsize hand, like lightless lanterns. He makes a fuss over clearing the gravel and sticks from the path with the toes of his gardening boots. Then he stands with his back to me in the middle of the road to look both ways for trucks. You cannot see around these steep bends in the road, he says, and where I have parked is bookended by bends, the road bends both ways. I nod. He says, "You know where you're going?" I am confident that I do, but it never hurts to hear directions a second time, as long as I do not invert them. With one empty glass he gestures toward the southbound bend, conducts his arm east, then west, and together we imagine the landscape I will traverse. Then I get into the car and roll down the window because he is still standing there with the empty glasses and seems to have something more to say. I cannot see his face in the dark. I detect only his shadow and the glint of glassware and the red plaid pattern of his shirt, which I know to be red only because it is still red in my memory of earlier this afternoon. He asks if I will send him the assignment once I have written it. He's curious, he says, to see the sort of impression he gives. He is like a person who wishes the barber to turn him round so he can see his new cut in the mirror. Do I promise that I will send the assignment along? I promise. Although I warn: I am not very good at these assignments the professor gives. "Well," the musician says. "You didn't start with much." Meaning that he, as a subject, does not amount to much. I assure him that he does. Very much. Then I pull away from the gravel and onto the road, between both bends. Maybe I will come back sometime and deliver the assignment in person, I think. We'll read it over orange juice. Then I realize I have forgotten the professor's instructions once again.

I roll down the window. "What do you think of this election season!" "What?" "The election!" "What?" "The election season!" "What of it?" "What do you think about it!" The musician taps the two empty glasses together to make a clear sound that rings through the pines and the garden with its soon-to-be-harvested squash.

He says, "If you lead a cow to a barn, it will choose a pen."

I think about this the whole way home. It gets lodged in my mind. I try to find the switch, the rhetorical flip, that makes this riddle transform, like a duck-rabbit, into the alternate rendition of itself. "Cows and barns and pens. Cows and barns and pens." I say it again and again out loud to myself in the car. For repetition is a way to remember, I have learned, as well as a way to coax forth the meaning where at first there seems to be nothing at all. "Cows and barns and pens." I am looking for the meaning behind the musician's adage so intently that I begin to lose my way. After a few miles I recognize nothing beyond the dash, and the road is going up where I know it should descend. I cross a river that I cannot name and should not have to cross. I turn around. There is no shortcut. I will have to retrace the exact same path. "Cows and barns and pens." Growing up, we called puzzles like the duck-rabbit illusion the "Seeing Eye Game." But as you can tell, it is no game. It is a trapdoor that leads you deep into the mountains of your own mind. "Cows and barns and pens." The driving seems slower the second time around, when I have already driven the road before, though in the dark it all looks slightly different. For a moment I am afraid I have made yet another error in navigation, and then I pass the recording studio again. I have retraced my steps. I think to stop for further directions, further instructions, for orange juice. I slow the car. The musician is enjoying the quiet of his garden in the dark. His shadow moves among the stones and vines and autumn squash that always seem to hold such promise before they are cleaved. He lifts stones and adds them to the low garden wall. I watch. I have a great desire to ask him what wisdom there is to be found in this riddle of cows and barns and pens, but I do not. I linger for a moment. Then I leave him to his task and drive away. For certainty is difficult to come by, these days, and I am reluctant to ruin it all. Beliefs are such a comfort to other people until you ask them to explain.

DISPATCHES FROM BERLIN

A VISIT

Today the phone rang—twice. I didn't pick up. I tend to avoid the phone, I think. Maybe even more than I avoid people. Though in the end it's hard to say which element of the conversation I fear more, the phone or the people who call. If I had to guess, I would say the phone. Or maybe it's the people? It's true that when the phone rang just now, I was disinclined to find out who was calling. To see the identity of the avoided flit across the screen only brings on a worse kind of guilt, I find, when still I ignore the call. Which is why out here, on the narrow balcony, abreast the flower box, I simply pretend I do not hear it when, for the third time now, the receiver registers a ring. I stay right where I am, enjoying an uninterrupted spell of ignorance. Then I hear a yell from the street. The voices are low, a little abashed. That is my name, I think, that's being shouted! Once, twice. I pause. I notch the cigarette into a groove in the tray. Then I peer over the balcony edge, around the fragrant wisteria, just in time to see the backs of the heads of two very dear friends of mine, friends who are even dearer to each other than they are to me—they have been engaged for years, the wedding keeps getting delayed—disappear around the *Späti* at the end of the block. That is the sound barrier of my own voice, I discover: the length of a block. I wave. Back home, on Eighth Avenue, it's likely my voice would have carried one and a half blocks, even two. Necessary adjustments will have to be made. Here people are gone, indifferent to you in the time it takes to walk to the end of a single block, not one and a half, not two. And to think we might have shared a cigarette—! Really, I don't know why I didn't answer when they called.

What if it had been you?

A CUP OF LIPTON

The oldest tea shop in the neighborhood really isn't very old. Established 1991. I go once a week. The shop carries jasmine in the grades of fancy, very fancy, flowering pearl, and deluxe. You can imagine which one I always buy. But today, when I come home with my small paper bag, folded over at the top and stapled just so, I am struck with acute regret. It seems to me some exquisite happiness has passed me by, or else remained stationary, like a ripe bud ready to pluck, back in the musk of the shop. It must be said: I am disappointed with my regular fancy tea. The sun slants through my window and through the windows of the apartments below, and I wonder how many people around me, in this very same sunbeam, on this very same block, are currently preparing for themselves the very fancy, flowering pearl, and deluxe. The tea sets of my mind proliferate on delicate trays with golden handles and friezes, and, like a woman eavesdropping on a party from which she was excluded—and indeed this is exactly the case—I look on with deepening resentment as the superior jasmine steeps. Of course, there was little to stop me from purchasing the deluxe, the very fancy, or the dull green and flowering pearls, with the caveat that these varieties come at double or even triple the price of the regular

163

fancy tea. Still, I might have bought one of these superior strains, only less of it, and so remained well within my tea budget for the week. But it isn't the same, to buy less than you'd like. To come home with an eighth of a pound instead of a quarter. Better to hold in the palm the full weight of the regular fancy grade that I have chosen. A quarter pound will last me through this Wednesday, at least, at which point I will resign myself to Lipton, into whose imitative arms I'll turn, come Thursday, once the jasmine has run out. A cup of Lipton will get you through the day. And it can be nice to have the sachet once the tea is drunk. The dregs find a second life in soothing a blemish or reducing puffiness around the eyes. Although, one ought to take precautions. Once, when I was trying to make a blemish disappear, I left on my forehead a rather too saturated sachet for rather too long—perhaps I even dozed off—and later, when it was time to go to meet a date for dinner, I found I'd acquired a dark stain above my eye that no amount of soap could mute. It was a bruise-like stain that lasted for days. It drew attention to my head. The date, by the way, went very well. The man I met was charmed and made copious eye contact—or perhaps he was only staring at my Lipton bruise. "I have to ask," he said. "What is this on your face?" He reached across the hen carcasses that languished on the table. "I love it," he said. "I can't stop looking at you." He thought the stain was the most wonderful thing about me, for a few hours he may have even fallen in love, and what would you have done, in my position? How could I have possibly told him it was only a temporary mark, that in fact I was not so unique or deluxe as he imagined me to be? And indeed his enthusiasm began to wane. It was fading by the second date or maybe the third, once the stain had vanished and I was drinking fancy jasmine, instead of Lipton, and looking quite myself again.

RE: RULES

In a book I adore a woman writes:

1.   Do not write more than once per month.
2.   Never mention the past.

A LOOPHOLE

Perhaps I will write to you every day and collate my dispatches into one.

SPIELPLATZ

It is astonishing, really, the extent to which the twins are not the same. The little boy chases a ball across the park, a streak of red delight. Later he runs his fingers through my hair and tells me, Really, I must wash. Things are not so easy with the little Fräulein. She is uncanny, like a cat. Her watchful eyes. Today she installs herself in the window with a slice of toast and jam and asks, Is it better to take one good bite with all the jam at once, or spread it evenly so every bite has just a little bit? Girls are much more prone to tragedy, I find. They seem to know it intuitively: something is wrong with the toast. And then they ask and ask, like pressing on a bruise. "*Liebling*," I say. "You can always have more jam."

A PARTY

I am getting along with my mother better than I have in ages now that we are communicating across several thousand miles, via the phone. We talk about gardens. We talk about food. She wants to know, "What are you eating over there? What did you have for lunch?" Recently I called to ask for the chocolate sheet cake recipe she used to make on birthdays. Cocoa. Flour. Butter. Sugar. And cinnamon, my mother said. Cinnamon—the one thing everyone forgets. I didn't forget. I went out to the store and bought each item in the appropriate amount, including the vial of *Zimt*. It's still there, actually, among the other groceries, in the bag on a hook in the hall. It hasn't moved a bit. I suppose by the time I came home from the store I'd lost the heart to bake a cake. The will withered within me, like an old fruit. In the kitchen there wasn't a measuring cup or tablespoon to be found, only a scale for weighing out ingredients in grams. And it had been quite enough to produce the translations—cinnamon to *Zimt*, sugar to *Zucker*, chocolate to *Schokolade*—without converting the called-for quantities from imperial to metric as well. I took a deep breath. I stared at the scale. Then I retreated here to the balcony to keep company with the really luscious wisteria my *Mitbewohnerin* tends, and which seems to have grown ever more alive, ever fuller, in the time since I arrived, no matter how much ash—whole grams of it, I expect—I tamp into the soil. But I wouldn't know. Such matters are beyond me, in the end. This business of grams and cups and kilojoules, the density of wisteria blossoms, the timer on the phone that logs the minutes I spend speaking to my mother. "Did you make the cake?" she asks, as we approach minute twenty-two or -three. "Another day," I say. "Tomorrow," I say. "The party is tomorrow." Or maybe it was today? There's a thought. Perhaps that's why my dear, almost-married friends just called.

RE: SYLVIA

How stylish to finish work at two o'clock and join everyone then, at just the hour when the crowd, like a too-warm drink, is in need of freshening. And on top of this to pay the rent? Really, she sounds grand. It makes me wonder if perhaps I should have been a waitress. How different things would be. Oh, to be forever fashionably late, to have always some new story of rich couples fumbling with forks, and cash from tips on hand. Let me be the first to tell you: no one here is fashionably late, not even me. I wait with diligence at crosswalks here, one little Schumacher twin dangling from either wrist. In Berlin the signals sound aloud to usher the blind.

AN ARABIAN NIGHT

My *Mitbewohnerin* keeps plenty of different kinds of things to eat stored in the little armoire in the kitchen. I admire the variety. I often lift the latch and take a peek, just to see how things are coming along. On her shelf, I find the strange still life of two apples, a bag of yellow egg noodles to offset the beefy burgundy of stroganoff, and also a half loaf of bread. The Germans are really very proud of their bread. Also their egg noodles, if I'm not mistaken. Certainly I can see putting forth these egg noodles as an object of national pride. The blue seal is brand-new and the noodles are perfectly shaped into soft-edged waves, as if shaved away in short, small strokes from a block of waxy dough. If it were up to me, I would walk to the grocery this instant to buy such a package of egg noodles for myself. Only, it isn't up to me. On evenings like these, everyone is out by the Spree drinking pilsner straight from the bottle, and that includes the personnel from the grocery.

Automatic belts convey name-brand egg noodles onto the scales of my mind. Of course I support the early closing of the shops. I think everyone ought to have a day of rest. The only trouble is, my inner clock is still set to Eighth Avenue time, according to which the hour for grocery shopping falls well past ten. It is a problem of profound jet lag. Here, during the actionable hours of the day, I go for a walk. I open a book. I slip the bookmark from my copy of the *Arabian Nights* with the idea of reading through to the end of a chapter, the denouement, only to find that the story goes on and on, I am once more transported, the tales are tucked one within the other and always beginning again. Later, I think, I will go the store. After dinner, I think. I turn the page. Now the time for dinner has come and gone, and out the window I can see the dark and velvet sky. Perhaps I should go to have a beer myself. There's a solution. Pretzels and *Bier.* Then I really would be edging down the slippery slope to becoming *deutsch.*

A SALE

It's no picnic biking home with five kilos of *Schokomüsli*, I'll admit. Put even two kilos in the basket of a bike and things can get topsy-turvy. But I made it home, however inelegantly, and for a brief and glorious time this apartment contained so much *Schokomüsli* that I thought I would never run out. Take a long look at five kilos of any breakfast food and you will see what I mean. For days I lived under the assumption that there was enough muesli here to hold me over until December or into next spring, when my visa will expire. I thought perhaps I'd bring some home for you to try. But, in the end, *Schokomüsli* is no different from water or crude oil or any other resource drawn from kitchen pantries or the bosom of the earth. Life is hemmed in by scarcity on every front, I am reminded, once the *Schokomüsli* finally runs out. Probably it's for the best. Probably I would have gotten bored of *Schokomüsli*, in the end. I wonder sometimes, Will you too get bored? I pose this question to the wisteria plant. It wilts a little, absorbs more sun.

QUESTIONS

What happens, for example, if one dies over here while on an au pair's visa? Do they ship your body back? How much does that cost? Who pays? Who is morally responsible for those transactions that slip through the wide weave of the net of international law? Can you ship a body 1-800-COLLECT? Is that what socialism is, the power of attorney to ship a corpse on someone else's dime? How will I go? When will I go? Will it be in Tiergarten, on a bike, after spilling groceries to the path? Or in the Spree, caught in the paddle wheel of a tourist pontoon? What will they tell you? Who will tell you? What will they tell the twins?

A FREDDIE CIGARETTE

After a panic a cigarette can be nice, and the best kind to have is a Freddie. The only trouble is, Freddies can be very difficult to find. They are French, if I recall. Perhaps that's why. In France I imagine Freddies are thrown about fast and loose and sold on the cheap, but Berlin sings a different tune. Today, a trip to the *Späti* yields only further pocketfuls of Camel Blues. Come to think of it, I don't believe I've ever managed to procure a pack of Freddies on my own. I must have been quite dependent on a friend of mine who departed all those months ago, back when I was still smoking Freddies. He always had a pack on hand. He had very strong opinions about very small things, like the best brand of cigarettes, or whether summer rolls count as a lunch or a snack, and it's possible his preferences influenced mine as we smoked there on the banks of the Spree, passing Freddies back and forth. From time to time the current pulled a pontoon of tourists into view, and the tourists on board would wave. Once, my friend lifted a hand in response—the one holding a Freddie—and, as if on command, some cheeky flaneur on the upper deck bent against the rail and raised, into the late summer dusk, the high white moon of his ass. It was radiant, as I recall. Things like this happen, you see, when you are smoking Freddies. The whole world is more radiant with a Freddie in hand.

RE: BREAKFAST

I eat oatmeal for breakfast every morning here. It is really quite a production. Sometimes, right in the middle of a batch, one must add more water. Other times, more oats. I like to think I have a knack. Once, when I was taking language classes at the library, I came right out with it. It was, of course, a glancing truth, a slightly coded reveal. For muesli is not quite the same as oatmeal, in the end, although it is indeed related—I wouldn't turn up my nose, for example, at a pot in which oatmeal and muesli mingled. But at the time the question was posed to me, *Was isst du gern?*, I did not know the word for oatmeal as it is ordered—if it is ever ordered—here in the cafés of Berlin. Perhaps in some later unit one encounters the words for anglophone and Asian foods, like "oatmeal" or "mooncake." Perhaps someday I'll go back and learn. For now, I have stopped attending. I simply couldn't keep up. What do you do? Where are you from? What will you become? these strangers rudely asked. And it would seem the future tense is not for me. Here I am, fixed firmly in the present of a noonday kitchenette, clinging to the lower rungs of human knowledge. More milk? More water? Are the berries warm?

UNEMPLOYMENT

Who could have ever imagined I'd come to miss the Schumacher twins? All that snot. All those playdates. And now—all this extra time.

LATVIA

Recently people have been speaking to me most frequently in French. *Parlez-vous—?* they say, and I am forced to shake my head. Nein. Not French? Not German? What are you, then? they say. The other day, at the bike repair shop, someone posed this question of national origin only to answer it himself: "You are from Latvia," he said. I answered that, to the best of my knowledge, this was not the case. A pause. A brow befuddled. "I could have sworn that you are Latvian," said the German man. I was so sure that he was wrong. But this was weeks ago, and things are different now. Now, standing here before my *Mitbewohnerin*'s armoire, considering a little can of easy-open peanuts whose lid releases with a *pfft*, even I have come to doubt where I am from. Here in the dark, bracketed by the open armoire doors, I feel I could be from anywhere, it wouldn't make any difference at all. And perhaps I owe this rootless mood to the country my passport says I'm from, a nation forever staring into other people's pantries, reaching in an arm.

NEWS

Today astronomers have released a photograph of Earth taken from very far away. From the rings of Saturn, actually. They sweep through the upper half of the frame, a vast tan curve against the cold obsidian of space. The earth, meanwhile, isn't how I remember it at all. It is reduced to a round blue bead, harmless and pristine, whereas up close, when photographed from the vantage of the moon, for example, it has always struck me as menacing and grave. From Saturn's rings, however, the Earth is adorable. An ornamental button fallen from some stylish coat. One hardly feels sorry for it. The real object of sympathy, in the end, is the sacrificial satellite, sent out on a thirteen-year journey from which it will never return. Soon, I read, it will dive down to the dissipated surface of the planet at incinerating speeds, and so be reduced to dust. I wonder: Why not settle for the rings?

RE: INTERVIEW

You write that you, too, are thinking of moving away. Please don't. You are so wonderful as and where you are. How am I to imagine you in some new and unknown place, walking briskly by a strip of unfamiliar shops? Our old street suits us, don't you know, in the photo albums of my mind. But how nice for you. Good luck.

Forgive me my contrarian streak, but I have to disagree. Obviously you should wear the navy slacks and a plain white blouse.

A MANDARIN ORANGE

I have become the kind of person whose nose is always running, The kind of person I always dreaded becoming. She's snuck up on me, this woman, who is so sniffly, especially when she eats or walks too quickly in the cold, and the heels of whose socks have worn away, and whose pants never fit quite right. Yesterday, when I went out for a new pair of trousers, determined to reverse this unfortunate regress, I found that nothing I tried made me look quite as nice as the mannequins hanging from hooks in the street market. One pair was too loose in the legs and snug in the hips, another tight in the calves and roomy in the waist. I stood before the mirror and wondered what kind of woman the manufacturer could possibly have had in mind. Not me, in any case. I left the store without buying any pants at all. Though if I'd had to choose, were it a choice between one of those two pairs and walking half naked out onto the street, I would without question have chosen the pair too loose in the legs. It is almost impossible, in my opinion, to find a pair of pants with legs too loose. It is as much a matter of comfort as self-defense. I like to feel I have the necessary range of motion to dash away in the event of some unexpected threat— and the worst kinds of threats are always unexpected, one must always be prepared to dash away. Although dashing down the street, especially in autumn, is yet another activity that tends to make my nose run so unattractively. It interferes with the breath. It seems to me a nervous habit, an anxious byproduct of simply being alive. I genuinely hoped it would never come to this. That the very fact of living would so constantly remind me of my death. That it does makes me quite depressed. I suppose one cannot dash away from oneself, in the end. What I need is something light and cheerful—a floral skirt, not pants. A patch of sun, not lying supine in the dark. I slip a Kleenex into the pocket of the skirt, apply a shock of lipstick. Then I saunter out to the store in search of some ten-cent solution, which arrives, would you believe it, in the form of a mandarin orange.

A NEW BOOK OF
GROTESQUES

How had we turned out this way? My friend and I were plumbing disappointments over slices of cake. That was one of the best things about this country—people regularly ate *Kuchen*. It was normal.

Not so normal, alas, were our relationships.

"Are they that harsh with you?" I asked. Of those men who had recently caused me pain—I paused to take stock on my fingers, one, two, three—at least two were mutual acquaintances.

"No," my friend said. "On the other hand . . ."

It is easier, I find, to speak about certain topics in a language not your own. For example, the superhuman ability of some people to take a remark you've made, twist it like a steel pipe, and thrust the mangled weight back into your stomach with a thump: here you go.

"I think," I said, groping for vocabulary, "I *think* the problem is a kind of masochism. I sought out those people who could never be pleased, whose feelings for me grew around a seed of hate. Then I made it my goal to please them, one after the next."

Everyone has problems. My friend signaled for the check.

If this were a fairy tale, I might have tracked down those ex-friends and -lovers and asked them what they thought. A quest! In a foreign land! But this was no fairy tale. Or rather it was, but of a different type: I was on my very first sabbatical leave with a giant grant to research sixteenth- and seventeenth-century goldsmiths, in particular Christoph Jamnitzer's *Neuw Grotteßken Buch*. The fairy tales were in my work, not my life. They manifested in Jamnitzer's prints, woven into goblets and coats of arms, anthropomorphized in armored crustaceans carrying cornucopias of fruit. They wound round the gilded face of a clock. For the entire history of art history the elaborate collection had been dismissed as nothing more than accomplished frivolity, utterly devoid of an ethic or politics, not to mention a historical conscience—

No one was more surprised that I'd received the grant than me.

This is to say if I could have quested, I would have. Instead I was on my way to the grocery store with a carton of glass bottles to deposit and a birth control prescription to fill. Never mind that I was celibate. It was gray, gray, gray—no one had warned me how perfectly miserable Berlin can be in January—and I was using the pills mostly for off-label purposes, i.e., to skip my period. Once a month struck me as basically all the time. One has to preserve one's strength.

I took the route past the park, making up etymologies along the way, as was my habit—*Schicht* is layer, *Geschichte* is history, time is a mille-feuille pastry in a window display—when one of the very men I would hypothetically have liked to question came round the corner, looking distressed. The tails of a severed bike lock hung limply from his hands. I glanced back over my shoulder, amazed. How did he get here? I'd left him on the other side of the ocean. In fact I'd moved here in large part to leave him behind. Had he forgotten how awful we'd made each other feel? And now he'd been so careless as to return. I was totally unprepared. He waved the ruined halves of the lock.

"Aren't you going to help me?" he asked.

My ex had been in Berlin for nearly a year, as he explained over beers in the nearest bar. I was taken aback. He smiled cruelly, which is how I knew he was about to mangle my surprise. "Of course I'm in Berlin," he said. "Everyone's in Berlin. If you want to be original, try Riga." I was stung by the comment, jealous to learn he'd never tried to look me up. Those were the unwritten rules of divorce: if the one moves away, the other is obliged to avoid wherever it is she ends up. Furthermore, to feel abandoned either way. Cliché that I am, I said, "But you knew I was in Berlin." He shrugged and sipped his beer. I noted, with wounded satisfaction, that my German was far better than his.

So much better, in fact, that I wasted upwards of two hours there in the bar fielding phone calls to help him find his stolen bike. In return, my ex told me that I was wasting my life. He implied that I was a cliché, with my nothing interests and public funding and ignorance of contemporary trends. I swallowed it all as unthinkingly as a teenager might a pearly bolus of cum, and left the bar feeling perfectly sick.

Can you believe the mistakes I was already making? My friend and I were back in the café the following day. I ought to have pointed out to him, I lamented, that I was at least one iteration ahead in mass-cliché production, that it was *he* who'd moved to *my* current place of residence, that it was I who had left him. These stabs were the basic maneuvers on which our duels had thrived. Touché! He always aimed to draw blood. It was wrong that I let him, worse that I so quickly forgot why he did it, the answer to which was obviously to protect himself. From me.

My friend pushed her plate away. Outside, the street was cloaked in gray. It was three in the afternoon, and already night was beginning to fall. We listened to the sorry sounds of people schlepping by. Outlined in January's cautious luminosity, her profile nearly broke my heart. She took a huge bite of apple cake. Her cheeks bulged beneath high bones. She'd found herself in a similar situation once, she said, one where it seemed her opponent would always have the upper hand . . .

"Well, what did you do?"

It was at the party of a friend, she said. A certain Sylvia. They'd been close once, but a sudden chasm had opened between them. It was unclear why my friend had been invited to the party, given this geological event. But there she was. The apartment was chic but tiny with a long, narrow artery of a hall that branched into the ventricles of three small rooms, which on that evening pulsed with music and people and light. It was like one of those dreams, my friend said, where the hallway you're traversing keeps growing longer and longer and the door at the end ever farther away the more urgently you try to reach it. She set off through the crush of socialites. Half an hour later she found she hadn't progressed at all. The rooms she was trying to reach—and really something wonderful was happening within them, she was sure, chances at love and enlightenment and beauty were being snatched from the air—seemed even more distant than before. A moment later the hallway was empty, and she was standing alone with Sylvia the host, who was flanked by her famous, much older boyfriend.

"*You*," Sylvia said, like it was the first word of a curse. "I remember the first time I saw *you*." She was quite drunk. Her older boyfriend looked on with trepidation as Sylvia described having spotted my friend sitting on the library steps near the office where they worked. "You were wearing strange shoes," she said. There was something in the memory that gave cause for resentment. Now, at the party, she placed a palm on my friend's forehead and pushed, pinning her to the wall. The three of them stood there. My friend, the host, the host's famous boyfriend. They were all waiting for Sylvia to remove her hand, but the moment never came. They might have been three children playing a one-sided game of London Bridge. It was hard to escape. The host stood just out of reach. And few things are more pitiful, my friend was learning, than swatting limply at your captor's wrists. "Love, that's not nice," the boyfriend crooned.

My friend paused her story in the last silvery burst of light. She took a final bite of cake.

"What happened next?"

"Well," she said, very matter-of-fact, "I grabbed her, too."

The idea had come to my friend in a flash. Of rage, perhaps. She was angry at being made a fool of by this woman who held some secret grudge against her. She doubted Sylvia herself knew what the problem was. A dull pain gathered behind her third eye, beneath Sylvia's palm, and so in a quick movement, my friend reached out and seized her breasts.

"That's not what I was expecting at all," I said.

My friend sighed. "I didn't enjoy it nearly as much as I thought I would." She scraped her fork against the empty plate. "The point is, I don't recommend revenge."

I shuffled home through the early whisper of a snowstorm, resolving, for the umpteenth time, to be more like my wonderful friend.

Though my first thought when I woke up the next morning in my ex's apartment, far too early, was that I never would be like my wonderful friend.

The room was dark and quiet and smelled of sleep. The lofted bed brought the ceiling close, and the empty socket of a chandelier fixed its vacant judgment on my ex-husband and myself. If you could really call him that. A marriage that lasts less than a year might be better described as an annulment.

Outside, the nickel swell of dawn. It was time to go. I carefully descended and shivered across the floorboards, picking out my clothes from precarious stacks of instruments and books. In a previous life, I would have snooped around to see what he was reading, but that morning I had no interest—perhaps people do change after all. I stood in the door for a minute, considering the warmth and the smell of him. Then I was in the stairwell, buttoning my coat, grateful I hadn't jettisoned the birth control. That's the problem with living, as I always did, with one foot in the past. I never gave up hope that things would return to the way they'd been.

I didn't see my friend for two weeks after that. Life intervened. I caught a flu that left me bedridden for a week. Next time we should get sick simultaneously, I suggested over email. Then we could still hang out. *We still can,* she wrote back. *I have an extremely strong immune system.* I wasn't surprised. I was tempted to tell her to come round with juice and lemons and broth, but I still cared what she thought about me too much.

By the time I could sit up, I'd lost three pounds and was due immediately in Zürich for a presentation on my area of research. Or not exactly my area—no one but me was in the area of research that was *A New Book of Grotesques*—but adjacent enough that I'd been invited to share my thoughts on guilds. The panel was organized around the development (or not) of intellectual property law among artists of the Enlightenment. *Can socialist values be adequately expressed through mediums dominated by cults of genius? Toward what does contemporary solidarity flow?* The Swiss have funding for everything.

Having walked no farther than the hardwood stretch from bath to bed for over a week, I struggled to make it to the Hauptbahnhof on time. In the station, the salty undertow of currywurst colluded to slow me down. Nauseous and wheezing, I reached the platform just as the night train was beginning to glide.

Thirty minutes outside the city, I caught my breath. I found my cabin and collapsed onto the cot.

"*Hallo?*" came a voice from the Murphy bed above.

"*Entschuldigung,*" I choked.

My cabinmate and I went back and forth in German for a time before realizing we were both American. Then a certain cynicism set in. We spoke about our work. He was an architect. "Oh, architects never stop working," I said—I knew because I'd once roomed with one. "That's correct," he replied. In fact he had to work tonight. But where? In the lower bunk immediately across from ours sat the model he was to deliver to the Basel office in the morning. It looked very official, enclosed in a bright white box.

"Try the dining car?"

"That's a thought."

He was very stressed about this model and the work that remained to be done. He'd been studying, apprenticing, racking up debts and paying dues for nearly seven years. This was a big opportunity for him. Unlike most architecture apprentices, he did not come from wealth to begin with. His brother was in the Army, his father a vet and trucker who'd died young of a heart attack. They all of them had weak hearts, he said. He knew he shouldn't be surprised by the sort of person he was now forced to deal with daily, the associates who exploited assistants like him for years, underpaying and overtaxing them. But it was disappointing. I was just beginning to think there was something familiar in the hardships of my cabinmate's biography when two tube-socked feet appeared on the upper rungs of the ladder, introducing a uniquely shocking stench. I will be the first to admit that I was no paragon of human behavior at the time, but those socks left me newly amazed, putting all stirrings of déjà vu to rest.

We sped through Brandenburg. The architect took a phone call with a colleague back in Berlin. They were redesigning a museum façade, I learned. An exoskeleton for the original building that would lie within. The reading lamp in my berth illuminated my lecture notes, and passing streetlights flickered erratically in the window of the train. I idly reviewed my outline until the tube socks appeared again, this time traipsing down the ladder to the end. It was only then, when the architect was standing right before me on the navy carpet of the night train's floor—oh, poor carpet, what endless disasters and fluids it had seen, it isn't right to carpet floors in times like these—that I realized I did in fact recognize the architect. I was ashamed of my delay, also hurt that he still did not recognize me. It's true I have one of those faces that transforms dramatically, depending on the day, and that it was many years since this man and I had been friends. We'd roomed together, as you've probably guessed. It was he who'd taught me how to fry a perfect egg; how to fight without crying; how important it is to keep on top of one's laundry.

Those years returned to me in a painful rush. Thursday movie nights. Communal dishes. Pasta Fiesta: noodles plus anything that was about to go bad. It was very devastating for our apartment when he was not accepted to architecture school the first time round. I'd tried to remind him that plenty of brilliant people end up applying twice. I found a letter by Henry James: "You will do all sorts of things yet, and I will help you. The only thing is not to melt in the meanwhile." I knew better than to stick it to the fridge. He slipped away into a bitter depression, eschewing movie nights and communal pastas of any sort, until it seemed we hardly even saw each other in our two-bedroom railroad. We were two more trains passing in the night. I hardly knew if he was alive. One morning, I stormed into his room, not caring if I caught him doing who knows what. "*You!*" I could have pinned his forehead to the wall. "*You*," I said, "have too much talent to waste! Do your laundry and get out of bed!" There was a rule in our apartment, given our platonic situation, that you always knocked. It is a good rule for any living arrangement, but one about which we were especially strict. He was pissed. I'd found him shirtless in bed, the window open to let the stench out and the winter in. A slow, cruel smile spread across his face. "What's this?" he said. "A pep talk?" A monologue that began this way could not end well for us, I knew. Yet I stood frozen, as if under some spell. He was sick of women like me, he said. Women who skipped through life tilting quotas away from him. He casually stretched his arms overhead, flashing the dark of his pits. The exaggerated gesture revealed just how shocked he himself was by the depths of his resentment. But it was too late to turn back. "After all," he said. We'd ridden violent waves to the land of Milk and Honey. What right had such mermaids to monopolize the attention of the admissions officers? What right had we to—? I grabbed the nearest book, a coffee-table edition of Bauhaus principles that I'd gotten for his twenty-first birthday, a truly expensive gift, and threw it as hard as I could. It was a fight to end fights. Or at least our friendship. In the resulting scuffle, I punched his exposed pectoral, just above the genetically weakened heart, with a force and conviction that alarmed us both. Ten years later, the slap of my knuckles against his skin returned to me with perfect pitch.

The architect pulled on his shoes without untying them and lifted the model from the cot. He cradled the white case to his chest as tenderly as a wedding cake.

"Dining car for me—want anything?"

I shook my head. He slipped the key from the compartment lock. I cried out, "It's going to be great!"

He paused in the door, surprised.

"Your presentation, I mean. I have a sense for these things."

He worked the whole night and didn't come back.

My talk in Zürich was also a success. I couldn't have known that beforehand, however, so I arrived at the station a bundle of nerves. And regret. I ordered a coffee at the first kiosk in sight and came away even more thoroughly shaken: six francs fifty. The desk in the hotel room was set with a lamp and a binder titled *Useful Information*. I sent a picture to my wonderful friend, adding that they ought to include a note on exploitative Swiss pricing. Her response was immediate. *That's just what food is supposed to cost in a protectionist economy with a livable wage and high social trust.*

On certain winter days, my hair can take on a reddish tinge. These are lucky days, and this was one. I put on a green, high-collared dress and stood before the mirror to pile my chignon. Outside, the street filled with the contented sounds of people buoyed by social services and trust. I was alone. In quiet moments such as these, preoccupied with tasks like chopping vegetables, editing footnotes, securing a chignon, my mind often wanders toward the people I've lost. There is something mollifying about slicing onions or pinning up your hair. It leaves you vulnerable to regret. Perhaps this was why the third man, the one I was afraid of yet longed to see again, who'd broken my heart more thoroughly than all the others combined, had always preferred my hair down. It was he, in fact, who'd first mentioned to me the *Neuw Grotteßken Buch*. That's how I'd learned. And here I was, years later, studying it. Out of unrequited love or scholarship, I wasn't sure. I looked into the mirror. My mother had told me always to pin up my hair in professional settings. You had to think about these things. You had to appear severe and strong. I wondered what percentage of the advice I'd received in life was faulty. There is no advice, really, for getting what you want, except to recognize when it arrives. And then to hold on.

The scholars gathered in the library. No one was in the mood to chat. We crossed and uncrossed our legs, buttoned and unbuttoned our jackets. The moderator tapped a pen against the table's edge. As we filed into the lecture hall, I recited a few lines from Jamnitzer's epigraph under my breath: "Useful for everybody, for those who like art / . . . Those who don't like it can lump it."

I am not an impressive person day-to-day. But on a stage, with my slides, and my hair pinned just so, I assure you I am in command:

"*A New Book of Grotesques* includes sixty single-page etchings produced as inspiration for gold- and silversmiths in seventeenth-century Nuremberg. The extraordinary alchemy of styles in the Gothic scenes evidence Mannerist, Baroque, and Italian influences.[1] The creatures depicted here have escaped a child's nightmare. Armored shellfish and spear-wielding sea creatures coil beneath limericks scrawled on floating scrolls. Though best known

---

1   Wick, Peter. "A New Book of Grotesques by Christoph Jamnitzer." *Bulletin of the Museum of Fine Arts*, vol. 60, no. 321. (1962): 83–104.

as a goldsmith at the time of publication, Jamnitzer catapulted himself to the vanguard of the immoderate imagination with these engravings, enjoying wide circulation throughout the land—"

Next slide.

"Up until important work published by certain of my colleagues in the 1960s,[2] Jamnitzer's engravings were primarily received as whimsical dreams, a cabinet of curiosities amounting to no more than the fantastical sum of its fantastical parts. In *The Bug Market*, for example, shown here to the right, a robed vendor delivers a snail. Note the inscription: 'The Bug Market commissioned for this purpose / Take from it what you like!' Now look at images four and five. In these objects, kilned some fifty years later, one notes the same creatures warping the handles of goblets and the bases of candlesticks. Such figures, wrought from gold, must continually announce their beauty to the world. Their form is a plea not to melt them down.[3,4] They are arguing for their own humanity. And by open-sourcing blueprints for such heirlooms, Jamnitzer went beyond advertising his own talents.[5] *Plunder me to make yourself*, these etchings say. *Please, do not melt me down*, say the objects that result. The cast is an existential argument that the *objet d'art* is worth more than its weight in bullion. And this is the same tension, I argue, of the individual placed in her social context. We make ever more elaborate plans to justify our existence in the face of all that came before."

---

2   Bakhtin, Mikhail. *Rabelais and His World.* (MIT Press, 1968).

3   Brisman, Shira. "Christoph Jamnitzer's Speechless Defense of the Goldsmith's Strengths." *Zeitschrift für Kunstgeschichte*, vol. 83, no. 3 (2020): 385–405.

4   Brisman, Shira. "Contriving Scarcity: Sixteenth-Century Goldsmith-Engravers and the Resources of the Land." *West 86th.* vol. 27, no. 2 (2020): 147–196.

5   Viljoen, Madeleine. "Christoph Jamnitzer's 'Neuw Grotteßken Buch,' Cosmography, and Early Modern Ornament." *The Art Bulletin.* vol. 98, no. 2 (2016): 213–236.

I clicked forward to the end of my slides, feeling for all the world like a figurine struggling to justify her existence against the poverty of her form.

The thing to do is not to melt in the meanwhile.

Applause.

My friend and I spent the rest of the winter nibbling cakes and flipping through reproductions from *A New Book of Grotesques*. We met in the café nearly every day, as if time were running out. I brought copies of rare prints. Whole afternoons slipped away in the gray light and the diseased air—the general malaise of late February. Together, we investigated. We studied the prints for hours, our cheeks nearly touching as we searched for details no one had noticed before. She had a child's capacity for fascination, my friend, and yet nothing about her was harmless. Her attention was disfiguring. It made me want to start over on myself. Our heads bent low over these ornaments, I was overwhelmed by regret over the person who'd first mentioned to me the *Neuw Grotteßken Buch*. My friend flipped to a goblet opened wide to the world.

"I'd drink from that."

I told her about my talk, about what I'd said of the effort to assert the value of one's form. It was an existential argument. The gray of the street merged with her face. She too had a very mercurial face. It was the source of formal problems of her own. She looked at the goblet. I got up to order more hot water for the tea dregs. We were at our favorite table, sharing our favorite cake at our favorite café, leafing through the pages of our favorite book. I didn't want the afternoon to end. When I returned, she sat in profile, lost somewhere out the window. I had the terrible feeling that she was disappearing right before me, slowly becoming someone else. Of course she was. We all were. I set the teapot down. The corners of her eyes tightened, as if she'd experienced a sudden pain. The café was very feminine, trading in cakes and candles and vases and décor.

"Let's get out of here," she said.

We left just as the snow was beginning to fall. On the boulevard, I turned, surprised to find my friend was already halfway down the block.

"Wait!" I called.

She stopped. A silence passed.

"Tomorrow," I said, "do you have plans?"

"Of course tomorrow."

Then she disappeared into the white. I watched her go. Who knew what she meant. I fixed her image in my mind. All that mattered, I thought, was that we'd find each other again.

ACKNOWLEDGEMENTS

The sentence "We carry death within us like a stone within a fruit" (p. 18) is modified from Michael Hulse's translation of *The Notebooks of Malte Laurids Brigge* by Rainer Maria Rilke.

The story "A New Book of Grotesques" was inspired by scholarship by the art historian Shira Brisman. The epigraph to Christoph Jamnitzer's *A New Book of Grotesques* (p. 185) is modified from a translation by Peter A. Wick.

Many of these stories first appeared in magazines to whose editorial boards I am indebted. "Honeymoon" and "The Party" first appeared in *The Paris Review*, "Dispatches from Berlin" in *Tin House*, "Siberia" in *Harper's*, and "Rumpel" in *The Baffler*.

I would like to thank the friends, family members, and strangers who helped to shape this collection; thank you especially to those who shared their experiences with me during my research for the titular story. I would also like to thank my editor Jeremy M. Davies, my agent Chris Clemans, and the entire team at And Other Stories. I am further grateful to Daniel Lefferts, Elina Alter, Lance Anderson, and Kay Zhang. Finally, thank you to my husband and first reader, Siddhartha Sinha.

Dear readers,

As well as relying on bookshop sales, And Other Stories relies on subscriptions from people like you for many of our books, whose stories other publishers often consider too risky to take on.

Our subscribers don't just make the books physically happen. They also help us approach booksellers, because we can demonstrate that our books already have readers and fans. And they give us the security to publish in line with our values, which are collaborative, imaginative and 'shamelessly literary'.

All of our subscribers:

- receive a first-edition copy of each of the books they subscribe to
- are thanked by name at the end of our subscriber-supported books
- receive little extras from us by way of thank you, for example: postcards created by our authors

BECOME A SUBSCRIBER,
OR GIVE A SUBSCRIPTION TO A FRIEND

Visit andotherstories.org/subscriptions to help make our books happen. You can subscribe to books we're in the process of making. To purchase books we have already published, we urge you to support your local or favourite bookshop and order directly from them – the often unsung heroes of publishing.

OTHER WAYS TO GET INVOLVED

If you'd like to know about upcoming events and reading groups (our foreign-language reading groups help us choose books to publish, for example) you can:

- join our mailing list at: andotherstories.org
- follow us on Twitter: @andothertweets
- join us on Facebook: facebook.com/AndOtherStoriesBooks
- admire our books on Instagram: @andotherpics
- follow our blog: andotherstories.org/ampersand